DARK WATERS

♠ ♠ ♠

Also From Cohesion Press

Horror:

SNAFU: An Anthology of Military Horror
– eds Geoff Brown & Amanda J Spedding
SNAFU: Heroes
– eds Geoff Brown & Amanda J Spedding
The Gate Theory – Kaaron Warren
Carnies – Martin Livings

Sci-Fi/Thriller:
Valkeryn 2 – Greig Beck

Family:
Magoo Who? – Anne Carmichael
May I Be Frank? – Anne Carmichael
Guardian of the Sky Realms – Gerry Huntman

Coming Soon From Cohesion Press

SNAFU: Wolves at the Door
SNAFU II: Survival of the Fittest
Blurring the Line – ed. Marty Young

DARK WATERS

A NOVELLA

BY

DEBORAH SHELDON

♠ ♠ ♠

INCLUDES BONUS NOVELLA
RONNIE AND RITA

Cohesion Press

2014

Dark Waters

© Deborah Sheldon 2014
Ronnie and Rita © Deborah Sheldon 2013

ISBN
Print: 978-0-9925581-5-4
Kindle: 978-0-9925581-7-8

Cover Art © Dean Samed/Conzpiracy Digital Arts

Internal Layout by Cohesion Editing and Proofreading
Set in Palatino Linotype

Cohesion Press
Bendigo
Australia

www.cohesionpress.com

For Allen and Harry

1

Brendan Reilly's ex-wife didn't believe a word he was saying. That's the problem with trying to start afresh. Sighing, he grabbed his glass of beer and took a drink. Nicole gave a jeering laugh.

"Beer doesn't count?" she said.

"Not all piss, I told you, just the hard stuff."

"You're so full of shit."

"I haven't had whisky in a month, I swear. No pills either."

She turned her face. "Whatever."

Brendan followed her gaze. She seemed to be looking at the meals counter on the other side of the pub's bistro. A staff member was taking an elderly couple's order. It was just on midday. The place was as big as a barn with the same cream walls, red carpet and brown furniture that Brendan remembered from when they used to come here as a family.

But the kids' playroom that Max had toddled around in was gone, replaced with pokie machines. An older man wearing a fluorescent orange shirt and navy workpants had been feeding coins into two different machines the whole time Brendan and Nicole had been seated. Brendan wondered how much money the man had already lost. The space taken by the machines used to be the exit point for a giant yellow slide. *Do it again, Daddy? Do it again?* Max used to tumble out of that slide, giggling, landing on the mat in a tumble of chubby arms and legs.

"How's Max?" Brendan said.

"Fine."

"What grade's he in now?"

'Take a guess."

"Don't be like that."

"Like what?" Nicole raked her fingers through bleached hair, tucked loose strands behind her ears, crossed her arms and stared at him. He waited. After a while, she said, "He's in grade one."

"Doing all right?"

"Yeah, his reading's coming along. His teacher likes him, reckons he's great at maths. He sucks at art, though. The poor kid can't draw for shit."

She smiled. Brendan smiled too. He wanted to reach out and touch her. Wanted to ask if Max ever mentioned him. Instead, he studied his beer glass, turning it around and around on the table top. On the second knuckle of his right hand lay the tiny white scar, thin as a cat scratch, and he found himself staring at it. It was this particular scar that had finally made him call her last night after so many years, and ask her to meet him for a drink. Miraculously, she'd agreed. Nicole had a matching scar bisecting her left eyebrow. He tried to brush the memory away.

"If you want, I could take you both out to tea one night," he said.

Nicole didn't say anything.

Brendan continued, "You like Vietnamese, right? Sure, you do, I remember. Those noodle soups with the chilli? No worries. Okay, what about Max? Does he eat that stuff? I guess he'd like spring rolls. I mean, who doesn't?"

Nicole sipped at her glass of orange juice.

"You seeing someone?" he said.

She sat back in her chair, put down the glass, her face closed. Brendan looked over at the man on the pokies, still feeding coins and shoving at buttons, playing a game he couldn't win. Jesus, the sight alone made Brendan feel tired and old, sick in the guts.

"Tell me about Max," he said.

"What do you want to know?"

Brendan shrugged. "Uh, does he like football?"

"Not AFL. I've tried him with a few different sports and he likes soccer the best. Actually, he's been playing in a local team since Easter."

"Oh, yeah? What position?"

"Goalie, mostly, but he's happy with any kind of defence. For some reason, he doesn't like attacking."

Brendan dropped his gaze to the beer glass. Their matching scars were from when he'd hit her that single awful time, when he'd been drunk and hopped up on speed, angry from work, stripped raw from Max crying all the time, frustrated by Nicole's refusals in bed, her exhaustion, her tears, her nagging. In the kitchen that night, during the argument, she'd pushed him. Two hands flat on his chest. Not even a hard push. A push from a short, slightly-built woman, a push that hadn't even unbalanced him...

He didn't deserve a second chance.

But lately, every time he looked at the scar on his knuckle he thought of Nicole, of how much he loved her and Max, of how badly he'd screwed up. That scar summarised everything good and bad in his life; everything precious and everything lost.

"You okay?" Nicole said.

He glanced up. Her look of concern made him realise that his eyes had filled with unshed tears. Embarrassed, he blinked hard. The accident had somehow knocked something loose inside him. He didn't understand it.

"This fucken air conditioning," he said.

Follow the bubbles.

His eyes were open but the bubbles were dark on dark, invisible. The world turned without gravity, a viscous swirl, neither up nor down.

Follow the bubbles.

Were his eyes open?

He couldn't tell.

Just try. Open your eyes and try.

A booming noise started. The noise ballooned from his chest into his neck, pushed up into his head and pressed against the bones of his skull, the force of it threatening to burst through his eardrums, split the skin of his face. He came to realise that the booming noise was his heart, clamouring and panicking.

His eyes were open. There were no bubbles.

A scream wanted to come out but the dark forced itself into his nose and mouth, tasting like dirt. He was about to die. That much was clear. The darkness squeezed tight as a caul and began to suffocate him.

Brendan kicked and thrashed at the caul. Gasping, sucking in great draughts of air, he sat up, disoriented. The first thing he recognised in the murk was the lamp next to his bed. The rest of the room came into focus. He was home, he was safe. It was just the dream. The same dream, again.

He wiped the sweat from his face with the back of one arm. As if the pressure could soothe his racing heart, he clamped a hand against his chest. At the end of the bed lay the top sheet in a knotted snarl. The digital clock showed it was just after three in the morning. He looked around at the rest of the room but it didn't reassure him. Naked, he got out of bed and went over to the single window.

His three-room flat was on top of a butcher's in the middle of a strip shopping centre. He opened the venetian blind. Milky light from the streetlamps bathed the T-intersection below. One road ran away from him in a dead straight line. At the end of the road sat the silhouetted Melbourne skyline and beyond that, the arched hoop of the sky. Nothing stirred. It seemed that everything in the world except him was asleep. He half-sat on the windowsill. The enamelled wood felt cold under his bare buttocks. Sweat evaporated across his back.

An open packet of cigarettes lay on the windowsill. He lit one and stared out the window as he waited for the adrenaline to clear. It always took a while. Time passed. He let it slip by, tried to keep his mind blank. Headlights peeped over the horizon. A car was coming directly towards him. Dazzled, he tried to guess the make and model from the beams. At the intersection, the car got a green and turned left. Too bad, he'd guessed wrong: a Hyundai, not a Honda. The after-image of headlights faded from his vision.

By now the kitchen and lounge area, little bigger than a garden shed, had filled with cigarette smoke. Brendan pulled up the sash window. A gust of late autumn air billowed into the room and ran chills over his body. Shivering, he stubbed out the cigarette and lit another one, then glanced over at the oven with its digital clock. Ten minutes had gone by, and his heart was still banging inside his chest.

Brendan decided to think about the accident. There was no getting around it.

Sometimes, he couldn't push the memory out of his head. Sometimes, like now, the only solution was to examine the memory in detail, one step at a time, and only then would it fade away. Of course, he didn't *want* to think about the accident, but if he hoped to get back to sleep, there was no choice. He mashed the cigarette into the ashtray and took a breath.

On that particular night...

The night of the accident...

2

He'd been driving home.
Driving his Holden Executive VT sedan with the sun-bleached blue paint and a radio that hadn't worked from the day he'd bought the car for three and a half. Crime doesn't pay, so the saying goes, and it was true for lowly foot soldiers like Brendan. For all the jobs he'd pulled over the years – and he was now in his late forties – he'd never made much financial headway. This was one of the things that had always irritated Nicole.

Forget about Nicole for now. So, on the night of the accident...
That night...

He'd been driving home from a meeting of the Overlords. A long and dreary pow-wow about market share, development strategies, fiscal forecasting, the kind of business that no-one had ever known or cared about some twenty-seven years ago when Brendan first joined the club.

Driving home at dusk, rain spitting hard enough to need windscreen wipers, Brendan felt tired. No, more than that. He felt brain-dead. For hours, the Overlords treasurer, Four-Eyes, who had a pair of eyes tattooed on the back of his bald head, had bored him and probably everyone else with his long list of numbers. To impress the club president, however, most of the officers had feigned a perky interest. *Screw that.* Brendan had been around for so long that he figured he could, without fear of consequences, rest his head on the tabletop. It took half an hour before the vice-president, Ellery Christensen, had finally tapped him on the shoulder.

Wake up, Ellery had said.

Brendan had answered *what the fuck for?*

That had got a few laughs. Not from Ellery or the president, though.

The windscreen wipers beat and squeaked across the glass. Brendan yawned. The narrow road stitched back and forth through bushland. Gum trees, colourless and ghostly in the mist, whipped past his sedan. On a good run, it was a half-hour drive back to his Hawthorn flat. A wooden sign, *Burleywood Creek is a tidy town thanks to YOU,* loomed into the windscreen and was gone again, a familiar sight.

What a crap little joint.

Somehow, Burleywood Creek was considered a part of metropolitan Melbourne, even though it lay so far north-east of the city that the area was mostly forest, green valleys, and parrots. The town must have been named after the local creek, a measly dribble of water that ran off the Yarra River, or maybe the creek was named after the town. Brendan didn't know and didn't care. Apparently, no-one else did either. Only a couple of hundred people bothered to live in Burleywood Creek. You just drove through it on your way to somewhere else. If you blinked, you'd miss the handful of peeling weatherboard buildings with a general store, cafe, petrol station and fire house that made up the main street. No post office, the town was too small for that, but not too small for the Burleywood Creek Hotel.

Brendan had been attending weekly meetings at that pub ever since his initiation into the Overlords. Back in the 80s, Jacko had been club president and things had been simple: protection rackets, bank jobs, and amphetamines. At the time, during what Brendan now realised was the Golden Age of Australian bikie clubs, who could have foreseen the speed of change, the fall of the old guard, the rise of the Eastern Europeans and the Middle Easterners? The new world had left many behind, including Brendan, who missed the easy camaraderie, the mateship, the do-what-you-want philosophy. Under the leadership of Stevan 'Vic' Petrovic, the Overlords had changed from a rowdy motorcycle club to an organised crime syndicate. We have to compete with the new bastards on the block, Vic used to say during those first years of rapid change, of transition. Brendan never understood that line of thinking. Compete? What for? The Overlords had been a fine club. Now it was... too different. No matter what changed, however, Brendan had always just shrugged and accepted it. Money is money.

On the night of the accident, Brendan was driving home from the pub after the meeting chaired by Four-Eyes. He'd driven the route hundreds of times over the past three decades. It was raining. This time there was oil on the road. Or black ice. Or road kill, smeared by traffic into a slick consistency. Whatever it was, it loosened the car's tyres. He turned the sedan into the hairpin and aquaplaned.

The lift and drift of the car had a feel that hit him first in his guts, second in his brain. At eighty-something kilometres an hour, more than twenty over the posted speed limit, the Holden lost its grip and shrugged its shoulder towards the fence.

Brendan watched the crash coming at him.

The barbed-wire fence screeched over the bonnet. Lines broke, snapping and twanging. The car dug into something, perhaps the gutter. Unexpectedly, the sedan launched into a cartwheel, turning end over end through the air so smoothly, so easily, that it reminded Brendan of a tossed pancake. The car took forever to complete its flip. Items in the console – wallet, mints, small change, debris in the footwells became airborne. Brendan wondered what would happen when the car hit land.

But it didn't hit land.

Sudsy curds of dirty water smashed against the windscreen. The noise came as a surprise. Despite the seatbelt, Brendan's head hit the ceiling. For a moment, he didn't know where he was. Something hurt in his mouth. His collarbone hurt too. A vision of Max briefly came to mind, the boy running, laughing. Then the coldness of water against his scalp shocked Brendan awake.

The sinking car made odd noises as the cabin flooded, a cacophony of whooshing, burbling and gurgling sounds. Dazed, Brendan couldn't fathom what was happening. He was upside-down, he knew that much. The seatbelt was cutting into his neck. He touched his face where it hurt. The dim light from the dashboard made the blood on his fingertips look black. The rushing noises became reality as freezing cold water ran over his eyes, his nose, his mouth.

He understood that the car was upside-down in water.

Properties in Burleywood Creek routinely had rectangular-shaped dams that ran alongside the roads. Brendan realised that he had flipped his car into one of these dams. But he could get out of it. Typically, the dams were only three or four metres deep. He pressed the seatbelt release, fell into water, righted himself. His fingers scrabbled against the electric button for the driver's side window. The suction of air leaving the cabin was deafening, the *blurp* sound popping his eardrums, as dark water consumed him. The water felt cold enough to seize his heart.

The engine cut out. The dashboard lights disappeared, the button died under his fingers. He didn't know if the window was open wide enough. Shoving himself through the gap, scraping his back on the glass, he jettisoned himself into the murk. He was now desperate for air. There was no air. He didn't know where he was. *Follow the bubbles to the surface.* But there were no bubbles. He struck out with arms and legs, swimming, hoping to find orientation. He was neither up nor down, suspended in blackness. His lungs inverted in on themselves. His heart boomed. The blackness squeezed.

The cliché of life flashing before his eyes didn't happen. Instead, he saw a moment with Nicole. A non-descript moment.

Summer...

They were in the backyard of the home they used to share, the three-bedroom house. His wife – a younger version, five or six years younger – was holding their baby, Max, on her hip. Max had a serious, wary, perplexed look on his face, as if something didn't make sense to him yet. *Shit, it's all right,* Brendan tried to say. *I'm your old man, aren't I? I'm your father. Don't look at me like that.* But no sound came out of his mouth.

Nicole's damp fringe was stuck to her forehead. She was saying something that Brendan couldn't hear. Anxiously, he tried to step closer. Nicole gave a sad smile. Max turned away his little face. Nicole began to walk off. *Hey, just wait a minute,* Brendan wanted to say. *Don't go. Don't leave me.*

They left anyway, faded from view.

Brendan opened his eyes. It was cold and dark. The dark forced itself into his nose and mouth, tasting like dirt. Brendan comprehended that he was underwater, that his wife and son had been a vision, a quirk of his oxygen-starved brain. He recognised that he was drowning, and was about to die.

His lungs convulsed one more time. Then a feeling of comfort and warmth came over him. Terror dropped away. His thrashing limbs relaxed. As his heart turned over, he gave himself to the dirty water. Nicole and Max had been everything, he realised now, too late. They had been the backbone of his sad and sorry life.

Thoughts began to fragment, detach and drift.

Then a freezing wind broke over his back.

Shocked, lifting his head, Brendan sucked air, and immediately started coughing and retching. Rain needled his face. He could see the gum trees whipping in the gale, and the broken wire fence, the grey clouds hunkering overhead.

Behind him, the black water released air bubbles from the submerged Holden. Panicked, as if the groaning water was a living thing, a monster that could drag him back under, he kicked and flailed to the water's edge. He dragged himself onto land. Barbed wire speared into his hands, his knees. Collapsing into the mud and long grass, he concentrated on nothing else but the sensation of the breath heaving in and out of his waterlogged body while he gagged and spat.

When his senses returned, he clawed his way across sodden grass to the asphalt. After a time, he managed to put his feet under him. He stood up. Everything hurt. He touched his collarbone. The pieces grated beneath his fingertips. The lancing pain confirmed he was alive. He looked back at the dam. The surface of the water was flat, calm, stippled by rain. There was no indication that the dam had swallowed anything at all.

Brendan began the long walk home.

He didn't mean to walk the whole way from Burleywood Creek to Hawthorn, at least twenty kilometres. That was never his intention. At first, he planned to stop somewhere and call a taxi, maybe even an ambulance. But every time the opportunity to seek help arose – from passing cars, from lit houses, service stations or 7-Eleven stores – he kept walking. He had to feel the world beneath his feet. The drizzling rain on his face, the wind at his back, the moan of overhead wires moving about in the gusts: he had to be alone with all of this. Whenever he tried to ask himself why, he couldn't get an answer. His mind lay blank. The journey took him nearly six hours.

At the end of it, a false dawn brightened the clouds. His three-room flat over the butcher shop had one door, the back door, accessible via a cobbled lane. Exhausted, Brendan shuffled across the square of concrete where his Holden would normally be parked. He hauled himself up the wooden stairs. His house key was back in the dam, hanging off the same ring as the ignition key. There was no spare. It took four or five good kicks to snap the lock. He went inside, and propped the door shut with a pair of boots.

The light in the tiny bathroom showed a corpse in the mirror. Silt, mud and blood covered the dead man, the whites of his eyes bright as spot lamps. Brendan stood under the shower for a long time. Death ran off him in sheets, swirling black around his feet, slurping down the plughole in a whirlpool. Finally the water ran clear.

Next morning, after a thirteen-hour sleep, Brendan emptied the Scotch whisky bottles and pill jars into the toilet. Then he went to the local medical surgery. Broken collarbone, black eyes, chipped teeth, an open cut across his scalp.

"What in blazes happened to you?" the doctor said.

Brendan shrugged. "I got beat up."

Day after that, he had bought second-hand a silver Holden Commodore VZ sedan for eleven thousand. When anybody had asked about the Holden VT, he'd told them it had been stolen from a McDonald's car park while he'd been inside eating a few cheeseburgers. Aw fuck it, he'd say, the radio was cactus anyway. That joke had made the boys laugh for a while, and then everyone had forgotten about his car. The Holden VT would stay in the dam, buried with the old Brendan Reilly.

Brendan thought about the car sometimes, down there in the dark.

He opened his eyes. Shivering, naked, he was sitting on the window sill, a burnt-out cigarette clutched in his fingers. Dropping the dead cigarette to the ashtray, he lit a fresh one and took stock of himself. Would he be able to sleep now? His heart had slowed down to the point where he couldn't hear it. That was always a good sign. He rolled his shoulders, felt the fatigue in his muscles, the sharp twinge in his collarbone. The doctor said it might take three months for the broken bone to completely heal. One down, two to go.

Brendan shut the window, took a last drag on the smoke, climbed into bed. The mattress felt good. He pulled up the sheet and doona. Sleep overtook him fast. As it did, he was thinking about Nicole, wondering when he should call again to invite her and Max out to dinner, wondering what she might say, hoping it would be yes.

3

Brendan pulled into the gravel car park of the Burleywood Creek Hotel. Sitting on a cleared block amongst a stand of gum trees, the hotel – known as the Burley – was a giant sprawling bungalow with a pitched tin roof and wooden veranda. Since the place was owned by the Overlords, locals tended to avoid it. Not knowing any better, out-of-towners still came in for lunch, dinner or live bands.

He took a parking space near the stairs. Motorcycles were becoming irrelevant to the Overlords nowadays – the Eastern European members, in particular, seemed to have no real interest in riding – but there were always a few Harleys and Triumphs out front alongside the utes and sedans. Today was no exception. He went inside. The place had panelled wooden walls, rough-hewn picnic tables and benches, a stone fireplace big enough to stand in. At eleven-thirty in the morning, there was a scattering of patrons waiting for the kitchen to open up. One of the barmaids, Rosie, gave him a wave as he headed towards the door marked 'Private'.

"How ya going, Danny Boy?" she called.

Danny Boy was his nickname in the club, given that his surname was Reilly. He supposed he looked Irish too: fair skin, dark hair, green eyes.

Pointing at the door, he said, "Everyone here?"

"Everyone but you. Drink?"

"No, thanks."

"Still not speaking to Johnnie Walker, hey?"

Her running gag; she'd been saying it for weeks now, from the first day he'd refused his customary Scotch whisky.

He pushed through the door, walked along the corridor, passed closed doors marked Cleaner's Room, Tea Room, Staff Toilet, Store Room. At the end of the corridor was an open door marked Boardroom. He went in. The club officers of the Overlords sat around a long, rectangular table, already talking business.

At the head of the table was club president, Stevan Petrovic. Women called him Steve, business associates called him Vic or Victor, everyone else called him Mr Petrovic or else. He was about forty years old and fleshy, ruddy faced, with greying hair cut short and neat as a banker. The room stank from his cigarillo.

Next to him was Ellery Christensen, vice-president, a skinny bloke with a ponytail and his teeth missing on one side of his jaw. Ellery didn't have a nickname, which was unusual. Brendan figured it was because of his demeanour. Ellery never laughed, never took things easy. You tried to make a joke with Ellery, he'd stare at you like you were a student in trouble and he was the headmaster considering whether or not to give you a caning.

Four-Eyes the treasurer was a genial enough bloke. He had two thick rolls of fat on the back of his neck, which at some point at every party would hold a lit cigarette, the tattooed eyes on his bald scalp glaring above it. That always got a few laughs, even after all these years.

The only other person at the table who mattered was the sergeant-at-arms, Itchy, a Pacific Islander. Itchy had ginger hair and blue eyes. According to rumour, on account of his white mother.

Everyone else was harmless, long-time patch members like Brendan, half a dozen men he could relax around. Four jugs sat in the middle of the table, three of them already empty. Brendan poured himself a pot and sat down.

Vic gestured at him with the cigarillo. "Danny Boy, we're talking about our tattoo parlour revenue. How are the new ones in Bayswater going?"

"All right, so far," Brendan said. From the pocket of his wool-lined denim jacket, he took out a thick envelope, tossed it along the table. "Two paid up, no worries, but there's one hold-out."

"Get it sorted," Vic said. "Today, take Itchy with you."

Itchy grinned. His warning shots were invariably damage to property, as in smashed windows or fire bombings. When up close and personal, Itchy never used a gun, preferring a cricket bat, pliers, and a little blowtorch intended for crème brûlée that he'd picked up from a discount kitchen warehouse.

Brendan said, "Hang on, the owner's a woman."

"Ah, it's equal opportunity these days, my friend," Vic said, and everyone laughed.

Brendan continued, "It's not this lady's fault she can't afford the weekly dues. She's already paying another club two grand per."

The laughter stopped. Vic's eyebrows drew together. No-one spoke. Brendan sucked at his beer for a while, careful not to meet anyone's gaze.

"The Golden Jackals?" Ellery said.

Brendan shrugged, nodded.

"Fuck," Vic shouted, hitting the table with his palm. "Those fucks, those fuckers, those pieces of motherfucking shit."

"Up to their old tricks again," Ellery said, and tut-tutted.

Vic stood up. "Bayswater is one of our territories, everybody knows that. Nobody goes into Bayswater but us. That was clear, that was made fucking-well clear to everyone, even those Jackal pricks. And everyone agreed. We shook hands. You remember that, Ellery? You remember us all shaking hands?"

Ellery nodded. "What did I tell you, Vic? I saw this one coming."

"All right, you saw it coming, fuck you, Nostradamus." Vic sat down, puffing and panting. Finally, he said, "So what are we going to do about it? I'll tell you what we're going to do. Hit Rashid."

"Rashid?" Ellery said. "You realise the backlash we'd have to deal with? We can't hit a president."

"No?" Vic said. "Itchy, you're the sergeant-at-arms. What do you reckon?"

Itchy sat forward in his chair. "We can't bend over for the Jackals. We did it once, okay, we're keeping the peace. We do it twice, we're a laughing stock. The Jackals haven't got the numbers, but our territory could go to the Angels, the Rebels, the Comancheros. Shit, maybe they all take it together and carve it up."

"Too fucking right," Vic said, and turned to Ellery. "Any suggestions?"

Ellery fished cigarettes from his top pocket, gazed at the packet thoughtfully, took out a smoke and lit it with his Zippo. Snapping the Zippo shut, he put it back in his pocket and took a long drag of the cigarette. Everybody waited, even Vic.

Ellery blew a stream of smoke, and said, "They breached the terms of the concord. On principle, nobody is going to like that. We can get the other associations on side, then sit down with the Jackals and sort it out."

"And look like pussies," Vic said. "No; if you don't want to hit Rashid, fine, then I say we hit Abby."

"Hitting the vice-president is almost as bad as hitting Rashid," Ellery said.

"No, forget Abby, I want to do someone in Abby's family instead," Vic said. "Give the prick and the rest of the Jackals something to really think about."

Ellery shook his head. "If we target their families, they'll target ours."

"Terror tactics are the best way to go," Vic said. "We're on the brink of war."

"No, we're not," Ellery said, "at least, not yet."

"What we need to do is strike some fear into the bastards. Let them know that nobody fucks with the Overlords. Now what family has Abby got?"

Ellery cleared his throat. "Wife, twin babies."

Brendan's heart became a knot. "Aw, come on," he said. "For two grand a week? We can't target civilians over something like that."

"And why the fuck not?" Vic shouted, his face suddenly a mottled purple. "Have you forgotten my nephew already, you piece of shit?"

Brendan recalled that some eight years ago, the Skulls orchestrated a drive-by shooting at one of Vic's family businesses, a service station. Vic's young nephew, Drago, an apprentice motor mechanic, caught two in the chest and died at the scene. Vic's crazed vengeance knew no bounds. The subsequent war between the Overlords and the Skulls had been quick, bloody and expensive – seven bikies dead, eighteen hospitalised with two permanently disabled, five in prison – but the Skulls were no more, wiped clean from the face of the earth by Vic's fury, their membership scavenged by other clubs eager to pick the bones. It had been a terrible time.

"I haven't forgotten your nephew," Brendan said, "but I haven't forgotten the war either."

Four-Eyes said, "And war is bad for business, Victor."

"My thoughts exactly," Ellery said. "Let's explore all the options here."

Vic took a final drag of his cigarillo and laid the butt in the ashtray. That was a quirk of his, never stubbing out a smoke;

instead letting it go out by itself. Brendan watched the tip of the cigarillo dwindle from red to orange to grey.

"Fine, let me think about it," Vic said. "Now everyone piss off. Not you, Ellery."

Brendan was sitting at the bar, tucking into a plate of chicken parmigiana and chips, when Vic came over. Putting down his fork, Brendan hurriedly dabbed at his mouth with the paper napkin and swallowed hard. Vic took a seat next to him.

"How's the food today?" Vic said.

"Good."

"You should try the goulash some time."

"It sounds too spicy for me," Brendan said. "I don't like spice."

"You don't like paprika?"

"I don't know what the fuck paprika is."

Vic's laugh showed off a mouthful of silver fillings. Then, tapping his fingers against the bar top, glancing around at the nearby patrons, he said in a quiet voice, "Listen, if we decide to take out Abby we need to tail him first, get a feel for his habits. Are you good for the tail?"

"Me?"

"Yeah, why not?"

"What about Itchy?"

"I need someone who's discreet."

"Sure," Brendan said.

"Just for now, watch Abby as often as you can, get used to his routine, okay?"

"Okay."

"All right, I appreciate it." Vic got up, made to leave, but turned back. "One more thing… the tattoo parlour in Bayswater?

That's your responsibility. If I don't get the two grand every week from them, I get it from you, understand?"

"Yep."

"You're a good boy, Danny Boy."

Vic began to walk away. It was now or never.

"Hey, Vic," Brendan said.

Vic looked around, slowly, his eyes hooded.

Brendan continued, "I know you're busy. Can we talk?"

"I thought that's what we did already." Vic approached the bar again, leaned an elbow against it, and waited.

Brendan said, "Look, I'm getting pretty old these days."

"Old? Are you shitting me?" Vic feinted a punch. "You're a fucking lion. Those biceps? You could bench-press me with one fucking arm."

"I want to retire."

Vic looked at him with a half-smile. "You want to what?"

"Retire."

"Retire from what?"

"The club."

"Retire from the Overlords?" Vic looked about the Burleywood Creek Hotel, taking in the iron candelabras, the stage, the vaulted wooden ceiling, all the while grinning and shaking his head. Then he said, "No-one does that."

"I want to get back with my ex-wife," Brendan said.

"So get back with her."

"She doesn't like the life."

"So get yourself another bitch." Vic shoved at him like a friend would shove another. "Come on, Danny Boy, you took an oath, remember?"

"I was a kid back then."

"You make an oath, you stand by it. That's how it goes."

"I know. I just figured because of my long service and everything..."

When it came, Vic's smile was flat. "You make me worry, talking this way."

"Maybe not retire. Maybe I could go from active to inactive."

"You mean be a life member?" Vic gazed around the hotel again, running his fingers absently across his chin. "How old are you, Danny Boy?"

"Uh... forty-eight."

"Forty-eight?" Vic laughed. "I figured you ten years younger."

"Nah. Forty-eight."

"You look good. There's something you don't like?"

"Huh?"

"About working under me?"

"No, Vic, nothing like that. It's just, you know. Just something I've been thinking about, that's all."

Vic took his elbow from the bar and straightened up. "Well, all right, now let me think about it. Okay?"

"Okay."

"Good boy." Vic clapped him on the shoulder. Then he said, "Someone will let you know about Abby. Don't forget the tattoo parlour."

Vic walked off, disappeared through the door marked Private. Brendan felt tired as all hell.

The barmaid, Rosie, approached. "How's ya lunch, Danny Boy?"

"Get me a coffee," Brendan said, pushing away his plate.

4

The oval had patchy grass and plenty of mud, goal posts at both ends, and a clubhouse next to a car park. Surrounding the oval were suburban houses, mostly old brick bungalows and weatherboards. Brendan had parked on the street some distance away. Close, but not too close. He lit a smoke and cracked the window. Frosty air seeped into the Holden.

The vice-president of the Golden Jackals, Abdullah 'Abby' Hanoush, was on his second lap of the oval. Abby had a loose, easy stride, as if he ran every day of his life. The only thing slowing him down was the dog he held on a long leash. Every now and then, the dog would fixate on something in the grass and come to a dead stop. Instead of yanking on the leash, Abby would pull up and whistle. The dog would lift its head, and the two would be off running side by side until the dog was distracted again. Abby didn't appear to get angry about this.

The dog was small, white and fluffy, some kind of Shih Tzu or Maltese terrier. Brendan had expected a breed more befitting of a Jackal: perhaps a mastiff, Alsatian, or Rhodesian ridgeback. Then again, Abby had children; twins, apparently, coming up to their second birthday, a girl and a boy. You can't trust just any dog around your kids. Children don't recognise danger. They pull a dog's ears; stick their fingers in the bowl while the animal is eating. Abby must have considered this when he chose the dog. Or maybe Abby's wife had made the decision. Brendan dropped the cigarette butt out the window.

23

Time passed. Abby and the dog kept running, stopping, running again. Brendan wondered what the dog was called. Finally, Abby slowed, led the dog across the oval to the steps at the foot of the clubhouse, and took off the dog's leash.

The dog started jumping and barking. Abby took a tennis ball from the pocket of his tracksuit pants. In anticipation, the dog raced onto the oval, yapping. Abby threw the ball. The dog tore after it, wrestled it against the ground, and trotted back to Abby with the ball in its mouth.

Brendan had wanted a family dog. Nicole had preferred cats.

At the time of Max's birth, they'd had a tabby named Pirate, his moniker due to a dark patch of fur across an eye. As soon as she had brought Max home from hospital, Nicole had worried that Pirate would sit on Max and smother him. She'd read it somewhere, cats doing that to babies out of jealousy. It got to the point where Brendan had given Pirate to friends just so Nicole could relax and stop checking for the cat's whereabouts every five minutes, especially at night. Lying in bed, in the dark, it had been all too easy to imagine Pirate curled up in the cot, a living cushion, purring, Max struggling for breath.

Brendan lit another cigarette.

After about ten minutes, Abby put the dog back on the leash. They left the oval and began walking along the footpath towards their home. From last night's drive-by, Brendan knew that Abby lived in a two-storey house that was brick on the first floor and weatherboard on the second, as if the second floor had been an afterthought. Brendan watched Abby and the dog retreat into the distance.

Sunday morning. What could be happening right now at Abby's house?

Maybe the twins were playing in the lounge room while his wife readied something for lunch. Abby would get a welcoming reception, the kids toddling over to him, his wife kissing him on the lips before castigating him about the dirt on his shoes and ushering the muddy dog into the backyard. No doubt, the washing machine would be operating. A young family goes through a lot of laundry. The sounds at the laundromat always gave Brendan memories of home. The water pipes in the walls had pounded and clanked as Nicole's washing machine moved from one cycle to another.

Abby and the dog were gone, perhaps down a side street. Brendan blinked, passed a hand over his eyes, then twisted the key in the ignition. Putting the transmission into drive, he hesitated. There was nowhere he had to be, no-one waiting for him. The Burley was as good a place as any.

Seven o'clock on a Tuesday evening and they were together, he and Nicole, in a Vietnamese restaurant, sitting opposite each other in a booth by the window. The place was large, crammed with laminated tables, plastic chairs, and diners. On the phone, she had refused his offer of a lift. He had arrived a minute ago and spotted her straight away in the far corner, looking pale and lovely, her blonde hair twisted into a loose bun, a scarf knotted at her throat.

Brendan handed over the shopping bag, and said, "This is for Max."

Nicole's grin showed Brendan, for the first time in a long time, those beautiful dimples. She took the bag and peeked inside at the cardboard box.

"Soccer Trainer?" she said. "What's that?"

"A bungee cord you peg into the ground with a net at the other end to hold the ball. You kick the ball, right? The bungee cord brings it straight back. Clever, hey?"

"Aw thanks, that's great, he'll be rapt."

When Brendan had called yesterday to invite her for dinner, he'd invited Max too. Nicole had declined. *You can't pick him up and drop him whenever it suits you.* So Brendan was on probation. Fair enough, he'd been a shithouse dad. His last day in their family home flashed through his mind's eye: furniture broken, Nicole crying, Max crying, then the police, handcuffs. Brendan glanced out the restaurant window at the traffic swishing back and forth on the wet road.

"I thought about Pirate the other day," he said.

She laughed. "Oh yeah: the mangy old fleabag."

"What? You loved that cat."

"Remember how it used to take at least one crap a day on the floor right next to the litter tray, like on purpose? The little shithead."

"Yeah? I don't remember that."

She shrugged and rolled her eyes, as if to say, *typical.* This annoyed him, but he knew he deserved it. The last couple of years of their marriage, he'd been flying high on pills, mellowing out with whisky, crashing and burning in between: a nasty, unpredictable son of a bitch. What had Nicole loved in him? He had no idea.

"Drinks, please?"

Brendan looked around. A waiter was hovering.

"I'll have a glass of white, thanks," Nicole said. "Sweet, if you've got it."

"Plain tap water for me," Brendan said.

When the waiter had left, Nicole said, "You still not drinking?"

"I have the odd beer these days, but no whisky."

"And no speed either?"

"No speed." Brendan put his elbows on the table, leaned forward. "Since I gave that shit up, I haven't freaked out, got aggro, felt paranoid, nothing like that, not once. Not even once."

Her smile was gentle. "I'm so proud of you, Brendan. I really am."

She touched his hand. An electric shock ran through him. Before she could break contact, he put his other hand on top of hers.

"I get it now," he said. "Everything you always told me, everything you ever said, you were right. Okay? I see that now. So fuck the club. I'm chucking it in."

Nicole sat back, pulled her hand free. "Will they let you?"

"I've been thinking about what I'm going to do instead," he continued. "Security work. There's training, these courses you can do, a few thousand bucks. I could get a certificate, be a bouncer, a bodyguard, that kind of thing. Have a proper gun licence. Put in a tax return and everything."

"Like a regular job?"

"Exactly like a regular job."

She smiled, sighed, frowned, and gazed out the window. Whatever she was thinking, he couldn't read it. Brendan imagined untying her scarf, trailing kisses along the length of her throat. At nearly forty, she was a gorgeous woman. She'd been much thinner when they'd met some twenty years ago, but there was nothing wrong with big pillowy breasts and full hips, a rounded backside. Women never understood how a man could want to feel smoothness, softness, beneath his hands.

Then he noticed that Nicole was still staring out the window, still not talking.

"Hey," he said, "what's the matter?"

The waiter put the drinks down on the table, startling Brendan. Nicole looked around and smiled brightly at the interruption.

The waiter said, "Ready to order?"

"Yeah, I'm ready," Nicole said, and gazed expectantly at Brendan.

"You order for me," he told her. "Whatever you choose, I'll eat it."

5

Vic lit a cigarillo and said, "All right, who's got the figures for Morwell?"

The secretary, Pinch, a man in his early seventies covered in faded blue tattoos, raised his hand. Then he put glasses on the end of his nose, took a piece of paper from his pocket, unfolded it, smoothed it flat on the boardroom table, and, adjusting his glasses, cleared his throat. While all this was going on, Brendan leaned over the table and grabbed one of the beer jugs. Pinch had been undergoing treatment for prostate cancer. Back in the day, he had been as hard as railroad iron and two-fisted, the man you always wanted by your side in a brawl. Poor old bugger.

"The new clubhouse is now rented with a twelve-month lease," Pinch said. "There's eight patched members, another six shifting to Morwell from Sale over the next month, and five initiates coming up to graduation. That gives us a total of nineteen by the end of the financial year."

"That's it?" Vic said.

"So far, yeah," Pinch said, and took off his glasses. "Not as healthy as we would like, of course."

"Any prospects?"

"Oh, I would say about a dozen, give or take. I can always shift a few blokes down from Mildura if push comes to shove. They could mind the club while the prospects ripen up."

Brendan took a long drink of beer. The meeting had already been running for two hours. The wooden chair was giving his buttocks pins and needles. Despite closed doors, the din of the blues band doing sound checks in the Burley's main hall reverberated throughout the meeting room. *One two. One two.* Twang of bass guitar. Flourish on the electric. Once upon a time, these club meetings had been wild and joyous – plenty of hard liquor, loose women, fun and games – but these days, Jesus, it was like sitting in on an accountants' convention. Brendan could hardly keep his eyes open.

Ellery was saying, "Rumours are going round about the Coffin Cheaters. They might have got wind of our expansion plans."

"Any threats?" Vic said.

Ellery shook his head. "We could try to head off trouble, broker a deal."

"And let them rebuff us?" Vic said. "Forget it. We keep our heads down and build up the Morwell numbers. Once we've got a big enough chapter down there to kick heads, then we'll talk with the Coffin Cheaters. Pinch, liaise with Mildura."

"Okay," Pinch said. "Mansfield is crowded too. I reckon I'll tell them to get a few members packing."

The conversation turned to the Overlords' recruitment drive. Members serving time were expected to size up other inmates as potential draftees. The Overlords had recruitment officers everywhere in Victoria, from the supermax Barwon to the minimum security Dhurringile and every prison in between. Competition was fierce. The other clubs recruited in prisons too. Apparently, fights broke out all the time.

Brendan took another sip of beer. *One two. One two.* A flurry on the drum kit, the rising wail of a guitar string getting tuned. *Two two. Twenty-two. One two.*

His thoughts turned to Nicole.

She had showed consideration last night when ordering their meal. For entree, she'd picked a share platter with spring rolls, chicken skewers, fish cakes and dim sims – foods that he recognised and could eat – and warned him that the dipping sauce had chilli in it. For mains, she got him a beef satay, which was quite tasty, all things considered. Nicole ordered one of those noodle soups that she liked so much, the kind with the vegetables, a little egg, and the crispy fried onions on top. The table had a basket with regular cutlery, but she'd opted for chopsticks rather than a fork. Impressive. *Show me how to work these things*, he'd said, and he'd unwrapped a set of chopsticks. Nicole had got up from her side of the booth to sit next to him, her thigh against his thigh, her hands folding and pressing his fingers around the chopsticks, the scent of her stirring his blood. He had longed to kiss her.

Something hit him in the face.

Brendan clapped a palm against his stinging temple. Startled, he looked around. The club officers at the table each wore a blank, guarded expression.

"Listening now?" Vic shouted. "Gimme back my smoke."

Brendan looked down. He saw the cigarillo smouldering on the table in front of him. *Son of a bitch.* He took a breath, tried to calm himself, swallow down his temper. After a time, he picked up the cigarillo, walked to Vic, and handed it over. Vic stared at him. Brendan didn't break eye contact.

"Okay, enough fucking around," Vic said at last, smiling. "Just dump it in the ashtray; I don't want it anymore."

Brendan went to stub the cigarello. Vic grabbed him by the wrist.

"Not like that," Vic said. "You butt it out, you make it stink. You lie it down and let it go out by itself."

Brendan set his teeth. The room was so quiet; it may as well have been empty. Brendan placed the cigarillo in the ashtray as instructed and returned to his seat.

6

Thursday was collection day.

Brendan always liked to start early, hitting the first business on his list at nine a.m. sharp. His collection area was the City of Knox, a shire in the eastern suburbs of Melbourne. A few of the suburbs in Knox, such as Bayswater, were mined exclusively by the Overlords. The remaining suburbs were shared amongst three other clubs. This usually didn't cause trouble unless one of the clubs tried to muscle another's list.

The businesses on Brendan's list were of the 'grey economy' variety; shops that relied heavily on cash transactions. Hairdressers, caterers, milk bars, fish and chipperies, cleaning contractors and the like had weekly dues ranging from five hundred dollars to two thousand, depending on cash flow. In exchange, their windows (and noses) didn't get broken.

Most owners were respectful, even friendly, accepting the dues as just another business expense. Case in point: Brendan always went to a particular cafe at eleven a.m., where the owner would hand over the envelope, then treat Brendan to an espresso and a bakery item on the house. Brendan might get vanilla slice, chocolate mud cake, apricot Danish or Berliner donut, whichever item happened to be the freshest that day. Then he and the owner, a big Collingwood fan, would talk about AFL football. Every Thursday, Brendan looked forward to the chat and the refreshments. Not all of the collections were like that, of course. Some owners were ingratiating; a few were fearful or even antagonistic, but it made no difference to Brendan as long as they paid up.

Today, however, he had altered his route. First up on the list, the new tattoo parlour in Bayswater that had held out last week. As a source of some anxiety, he wanted to get this collection out of the way as soon as possible.

He pushed open the door, which jangled a bell. The owner came out from the back room, a thin middle-aged woman with cropped hair dyed jet-black, heavy makeup, and a stud in her nose. She saw him and blanched.

"It's okay," he said, smiling, holding up empty hands. "How're you doing?"

She looked around the tattoo parlour, as if searching for something. Brendan looked around too. There was no-one else there.

"I thought I sorted this out with you already," she said. "I'm paying the Jackals. I'm not made of money."

"Tina, isn't it?"

She nodded, wide-eyed, white-faced.

"Listen, Tina," he continued, "you need to understand there's no choice. I don't have a choice either. How do you reckon it'd look if I couldn't get a little sheila like you to pay up? See my predicament?"

Tina groaned, sat down on the nearest saddle seat, and rubbed her hands over her face. Both of her bare arms had full tattoo sleeves, intricate designs involving green apples, lemons, bunches of purple grapes. When she finally looked up, she seemed drawn and ill.

"Okay," she said, "but I've got to go to the bank. Can you give me an hour? I'll have to close up, and a client's due any minute."

He checked his watch. "One hour. I'll see you then."

A misting rain had begun to fall. Brendan jogged back to his car. He spent the next forty minutes doing pick-ups around Bayswater, Boronia and Scoresby. Then he pulled up outside a shop that sold second-hand baby furniture.

This was a different sort of collection to the others. About a year ago, the owner of this shop, a man named Xavier, had taken a $30,000 cash loan from a friend as start-up money. The friend had spent the next eight months asking Xavier for repayments, in vain, before selling the debt to the Overlords. Now Xavier owed the Overlords $60,000 and counting, depending on the size of Xavier's weekly repayments. As Vic liked to say, Xavier was out of the piss and into the shit.

Brendan parked a couple of shops away and approached on foot. Xavier's store was glass-fronted. Brendan peeked through the window. A sole customer, a heavily pregnant woman, was checking out the prams. Brendan could see Xavier behind the counter, both of his hands visible on the counter as he filled in some kind of paperwork. Satisfied, Brendan entered the shop.

"G'day," he said.

Xavier looked up. He had a meagre comb-over and pale, watery eyes. He glanced at the wall clock, and said, "You're early."

"I know." Brendan approached the counter, unzipping his jacket. The shop felt hot as a furnace after the outside chill.

Shooting a worried look at his customer, Xavier reached beneath the counter. Brendan steeled himself. Xavier took out an envelope and handed it over.

"See you next week," Brendan said, and went to leave.

"Wait a second."

Brendan stopped, turned around.

Xavier said, "I need a rain cheque on next week's payment."

"You know that's not the way we do things."

"Everything will be back to normal the following week, no bull."

Brendan smiled. "Like I said, that's not the way we do things."

"Something's come up," Xavier said, his forehead beginning to shine. "In fact, a couple of things have come up. The following week, no bull, everything will be back to normal."

Xavier looked over at the customer. Brendan looked over, too. The pregnant woman had moved away from the prams and was now standing among the cots, rubbing at her giant belly in a calm, preoccupied way.

"She looks about ready to pop," Brendan said.

"Just one week."

"She's got a week to go? Jesus, how do you even know that?"

"I'm not talking about *her*," Xavier hissed, "I'm talking about the next payment. I can give it to you in one more week, just fourteen days from now."

"No."

Xavier shook his head in a helpless way. "What can I do?"

"Give us stuff we can sell."

Xavier gestured around his shop, the sweep of his arm suggesting that Brendan could take the entire contents if he felt like it.

"Nah, this second-hand shit's worth fuck-all," Brendan said. "You got a car?"

"What? You mean lying around?"

"Come on, you've got to have something that's worth a bit of dough. How about a boat, caravan, trailer, motorbike? A plasma TV?"

"Oh." Xavier seemed ready to cry. "Next Thursday, I'll have something for you."

"Thanks mate."

Heading towards the exit, Brendan almost bumped into the customer, who was making for the display of highchairs. Brendan pulled up to let her go first. She smiled. In return, he tipped an imaginary hat and grinned. Then he left the shop.

It was a few minutes after ten by the time he pulled up outside the Bayswater tattoo parlour again. He looked up and down the street, glanced through the shop window. The bell jangled as he opened the door. Tina stood bolt upright from a chair at the rear of the shop. Brendan was about to say hello when he realised that two men were closing in on him, one on either side.

Bracing, he raised his fists. The men hesitated for a second, giving him a chance to look them over. He didn't recognise them. The one in the suit had dark curly hair and brown eyes, slim build. The other man was larger, bearded, wearing jeans and a puffy sleeveless parka. Neither of them had a visible weapon.

"The fuck is this?" Brendan said.

"You know exactly what this is," the suit said.

"Vic's not going to like it," Brendan said.

"Rashid doesn't give a fuck if Vic likes it or not," the suit said.

The bearded man reached back. From his waistband, he pulled out a short club and showed it to Brendan.

"Not in here," Tina yelled, hurrying forward. "Holy Mary, not inside my parlour. You know how much I paid for the goddamned fit-out?"

"Aw, you cow," Brendan said through his teeth.

"What, you think I can afford to shell out four thousand dollars a week to all you leeching bastards?" Tina wailed. "You're lucky I didn't call the cops."

The bearded man and the suit advanced, slowly. Brendan's blood sang and whipped through his veins as he tried to figure out the angles. The tattoo parlour was claustrophobic; a tiny floor space jammed with partitioned stations, multiple chairs, jewellery racks. He had to get outside.

Flinging open the door, he made it two strides onto the footpath before he was kicked. He staggered. The bearded man's first swing of the club caught Brendan on the cheekbone, the second on the ear. He could hear a high-pitched shriek from somewhere close, over and over, probably coming from Tina. Next, a white-hot, dazzling pain burst across the back of his head, momentarily flaring his vision into silver fragments. He swung around. The bearded man was hauling back, ready to strike again with the club.

Drop punt.

Acting more on instinct than planning, Brendan kicked between the man's splayed legs with enough force to long-bomb a goal from sixty metres out. Beard launched into the air with a terrible *oof* sound before collapsing. By now, people in the immediate area were running, the strip shopping centre emptying fast. No doubt, cops were already called and on the way.

Beard was groaning and rolling on the footpath. Crouching, Brendan held up his fists, one eye already swollen shut, as the suit advanced cautiously with a knife clutched in one hand. Suit lunged. Brendan blocked, punched him in the stomach, hard. Suit let out a sharp barking sound, and then lurched away down the street, doubled up, retching, shambling as if on the point of falling down. Brendan was too exhausted to follow.

Tina's screams came to his attention. He looked over. She was standing in the doorway of her parlour, eyes bugged out, mouth open in a trembling, howling grimace. *Fuck you*, he wanted to say, but didn't have the strength. At his feet lay the knife, a switchblade. With some effort, he picked it up, closed it, put it in his pocket.

Beard was still lying with both hands locked between his legs, gently puking onto the concrete. Brendan knelt down. Unzipping Beard's parka, Brendan searched and found three envelopes, all of which he took.

"Arsehole," Beard muttered.

Brendan straightened up, and said, "This isn't over." Pointing at Tina, he added, "Not for you, either."

She shrank away, gibbering. A police siren sounded in the distance. Brendan slipped the envelopes into his wool-lined denim jacket, and limped towards his car. Civilians were peeking out of shops, from behind cars, staring at him in shock and alarm. He hoped that this particular shopping strip didn't have CCTV.

Getting into his car was painful. He didn't recall hurting his back in particular. He started the engine and decided to drive straight to the Burleywood Creek Hotel.

7

Brendan was seated in the boardroom with Vic and Ellery, the door closed. The envelopes that he had taken from the bearded man were on the table, emptied of their notes: five and a half thousand dollars in total. The story wasn't long and didn't take much time to tell. When he finished, Brendan fell quiet. No-one spoke. Vic was visibly angry, breathing hard, nostrils flaring. Ellery looked as unruffled as ever.

At last, Vic clapped a hand on Brendan's back, and said, "Good job, Danny Boy. You represented the club."

"Thanks, Vic."

"A couple of jackass Jackals can't get the better of an Overlord, right?"

"Right."

"You fucken betcha. Ellery, give him a drink."

A jug and glasses were on the table. Ellery poured a beer and handed it over. Brendan took a long swallow. His collarbone ached. Cuts on his scalp and face stung.

Vic turned to Ellery and said, "The descriptions ring any bells?"

"The one with the beard would be Farid. The other is probably Talal."

"That's what I thought too," Vic said. "Fucken shit-sacks."

"We've got to respond to this now," Ellery said. "Any delay, we look weak. I'll arrange a sit-down."

"A sit-down?"

His face reddening, Vic snatched up the folded knife that Brendan had taken from the suit, and threw it at Ellery. It hit him in the chest and landed on the floor.

Vic shouted, "What we do is return this fucking blade inside a Jackal's chest."

Ellery picked up the knife and put it back on the table.

Brendan said, "I'm sorry about all this."

Vic gripped Brendan's shoulder. "It's sweet, Danny Boy." He grabbed a hundred-dollar note from the table and stuffed it into Brendan's jacket pocket. "This is for your trouble."

"No, it's okay –"

"Shut up. You earned it."

"Thanks, Vic."

"The least I can do. Ellery, go get Itchy."

Ellery left the room, closing the door behind him.

"We'll sort these fuckers out," Vic said, "Don't you worry."

Brendan nodded. "Listen, I was wondering…"

Vic waited. "Yeah, what? You were wondering what?"

"If you've had time to think about what I mentioned the other day."

"What you mentioned?"

"You know… my retirement."

Vic leaned back in the chair, picked at lint on his polo shirt. "It slipped my mind. In case you haven't noticed, we've got a lot of pressing shit going on."

"Yeah, but you'll think about it soon, won't you?"

Vic grinned as if surprised, delighted. "Aw, Danny Boy, you're a tenacious little bugger."

"So you'll think about it?"

"You're like one of them mutts, what are they? A terrier."

Vic laughed. To be polite, so did Brendan, even though

Abby and his little white dog had just come to mind. This attack had sealed Abby's fate, Brendan realised, and he suddenly felt lightheaded.

The door opened. Ellery and Itchy came in and sat down.

"The fuck happened to you?" Itchy said to Brendan.

"Itchy, go sort out this bitch at the Bayswater tattoo parlour," Vic said.

"*She* did this to him?"

"No, shit-for-brains, the Jackals did this to him," Vic said. "They jumped him at the parlour after the shifty moll gave them the heads-up. Now go give her a manners lesson."

"What kind?"

"Your call, but she's gotta still be able to earn a living or else she can't pay us. And use a bit of discretion."

Beaming, Itchy hurried from the room.

As the door slammed, Ellery said, "You sure that's a good idea? Itchy wouldn't know discretion from his elbow."

"And that's why I love the dumb bastard," Vic said. Turning to Brendan, he continued, "Go home and take it easy. We'll be in touch."

"What about my collections? I'm only half-way through."

"Give the list to Ellery. Someone else can finish for you."

Brendan got up, dropped the list on the table, and left.

He drove through the narrow, winding roads of Burleywood Creek at a slow pace, the windscreen wipers on low against the drizzle. Fog curled out from between the trees in long, beckoning fingers. He wondered what was going to happen to the owner of the tattoo parlour. Then he thought about Abby. If Vic really wanted to send a message of terror to the Jackals, he would let Itchy off the leash and allow him to indulge his penchant for shocking details like severed ears, scalping, punctured eyeballs. Brendan shivered. *Relax, nothing's been decided yet.* He turned up the fan speed on the heater.

The road twisted and turned. The hairpin approached. Brendan slowed down. Without analysing what he was doing, he braked and pulled the car on to the dirt shoulder. The windscreen wipers shrieked across the glass. Dead ahead was the section of fence, still broken after all these weeks. The owner of the land mustn't have noticed the snapped barbed wire and splintered posts, or else didn't care enough to arrange repairs. Beyond the break in the fence was the dam. And somewhere beneath the water's shimmering skin, upside down, was his drowned Holden VT, the keys in the ignition.

A crawling sensation slithered up Brendan's back and into his hairline. The sensation was so strong, so physical, that he had to look around to reassure himself that no-one (no *thing*) was locked in the car with him, touching him with cold, bony hands.

He slammed the transmission into drive and took off, fast.

He was at home, listless, watching the six p.m. news on TV, when someone knocked. Muting the TV with the remote, he called, "Who is it?"

"Hey, it's me."

Recognising her voice immediately, leaping up from the couch, Brendan unlocked and opened the door. Nicole's smile fell away as soon as she saw him.

"Oh my God," she said. "What happened?"

Absently, he touched at his black eye. "Nothing... I fell over."

"You fell over?"

"Yeah, while I was jogging. Get inside. It's freezing out there."

She stepped in. He closed the door behind her and went to kiss her on the cheek but she pushed him away. With a fed-up and bitter smile, she slapped a sheaf of letters against his chest.

"I couldn't find your front door," she said. "The butcher downstairs told me to go around the back lane, and gave me your fucking mail to deliver, so here it is."

He took the letters from her and put them on the bench. She crossed her arms.

"What's wrong?" he said.

"You must think I'm stupid."

"Of course not."

"Okay, whatever. Fuck this for a joke," she said, and went to leave.

"Wait," he said, putting his hand on the door. After a moment, he continued, "Look, the truth is... I got beat up."

She turned to him. "No shit."

"I don't want to expose you to the life, that's all."

She laughed, as if surprised. "God, we've been divorced for years, and you're still trying to protect me?"

He shrugged, expecting her to start yelling. However, for reasons that he didn't quite understand, Nicole's face softened. Somehow, he'd said the right thing. She touched the side of his face.

"Who beat you up?" she said.

"Blokes from another club. I gave them the short end of the stick, believe me."

Nicole looked him over. It made him self-conscious. Dressed in tracksuit pants and nothing else, he became aware of the flesh on his hips, the padding of fat starting to blur his abdominal muscles. Despite cutting back on junk food, increasing the weight training, the running, he was getting soft; growing old.

"I should have called first," Nicole said, "but I was in the area and thought I'd drop this in for you."

She reached into her bag, took out a folded piece of paper, and handed it to him. He opened it up. It was a kid's drawing, a stick figure kicking at a ball on a rope. In a sudden flood of shock and gratitude, Brendan realised that it was a self-portrait: his son's drawing.

"The Soccer Trainer," he said.

He had to sit down on the couch. The picture was done in marker pens; the stick figure purple, the ball red, a lop-sided yellow sun in the right-hand corner.

"I told you that Max can't draw for shit, didn't I?" Nicole walked up behind Brendan and rested a hand on the back of his neck. "See the face in the picture?"

"It's smiling."

"He absolutely loves your present."

Brendan closed his eyes and said, "Does he know about me?"

"I've told him a few things."

Brendan folded the drawing, placed it on top of the TV, and stood up to face her. He said, "I want to be his proper dad from now on."

She nodded, offered a non-committal shrug.

"I'm sorry," he said, "for everything."

She nodded again.

He put his arms about her. She didn't resist. The long tendrils of her hair felt soft through his fingers. When he put his mouth on hers, she opened her lips. He kissed her deeply. After a while, he picked her up and took her to bed.

The world turned without gravity, a viscous swirl, neither up nor down.

Follow the bubbles.

Were his eyes open?

He couldn't tell.

Brendan flailed at the suffocating darkness, trying to free

himself, trying to breathe. Death was coming for him. Then somebody's hands reached down into the water and caught hold of him.

"Brendan," came Nicole's voice, "wake up, for Christ's sake, wake up."

With a start, he opened his eyes. He saw the bedroom ceiling, which disorientated him until he saw the digital clock: just after two-thirty in the morning. So he was at home. It was the middle of the night. Next to him in bed, propped up on an elbow, was Nicole, stroking his sweating face. For a moment, he thought he was still dreaming.

"Jesus," Nicole said, "are you okay?"

He took a long sigh to steady his hammering heart. "Yeah, I'm okay."

"What was your nightmare about?"

"Nothing."

"Nothing? Bullshit."

"Look, I can't remember, that's all. There were tigers, I think."

He got out of bed and lit a cigarette. Moving towards the single window, he stepped over the remains of their dinner: fish and chips. After they had made love and picked up the takeaway, Nicole had called her mother to advise that she wouldn't be home that night. Ever since the divorce, Nicole and Max had lived with the old battleaxe. It was Nicole's only option. She needed to work, and couldn't afford childcare. *My fault again.* He half-sat on the window sill, lifting the blind to stare out at the night sky, the sliver of moon. If he'd been any sort of decent bloke, he'd have provided child support from day one of their separation, the day he'd been arrested for hitting her.

"How much child support do you reckon I owe you?" he said.

"You mean altogether?" Nicole sat up, the sheet slipping down to reveal her breasts. "Shit, I don't know… a lot."

"Work it out and let me know."

She laughed, but good-naturedly. "Aw, don't tell me you're going to pay it."

"I'm going to pay it."

"Yeah, sure you are," she said, and laughed again.

"Dead-set, I am."

She sobered, got out of bed, put on one of his t-shirts and came over. Leaning against the wall, she regarded him with troubled eyes. He found that he couldn't meet her gaze.

She said, "What happened to you a few weeks ago?"

He shrugged.

Stepping closer, she said, "Was it bad?"

"Bad?"

"The thing that happened. Did you find out you have cancer?"

"Huh? Fuck, no."

"Then what?"

Shaking his head, he closed his eyes, dragged on his cigarette and crushed the butt in the ashtray, his heart racing.

Finally, Nicole took his hand and whispered, "Baby, why won't you tell me?"

Because some things just can't be shared. Some things have no words to explain them.

"Come here," he said.

She moved into his arms. He pressed his face into her neck and hugged her.

8

Brendan was having lunch at the Burleywood Creek Hotel, sitting in a booth and reading the newspaper, when Ellery joined him.

"We've sorted out your recalcitrant tattoo artist," Ellery said. "Itchy broke her off hand, with a warning that next time he'd break her working hand. She's willing to cooperate now."

"Okay. What about the Jackals?"

"They've been contacted, told to back off." Ellery shrugged. "Whether or not they will? Only time will tell. By the way, you put Farid in hospital. Excellent work."

"Farid? Is that the one with the beard?"

"Yes."

"No shit, he ended up in hospital?"

Ellery nodded, smiled. "Ruptured testicle."

"Christ. You know, I wouldn't have kicked him in the nuts if the bastard hadn't been hitting me with a club." Brendan took a bite of his steak sandwich. Around the mouthful, he said, "How do you reckon the Jackals will react to all this?"

"They're a proud club. I'd be surprised if they sat on their hands."

"Is Vic going to hit Abby?"

"I hope not. At any rate, I'm doing my best to talk him out of it. In my opinion, the best course of action would be to bash the blokes who jumped you. Farid and Talal. Perhaps shoot them in the legs; that would be another option."

With a sigh, Brendan put his steak sandwich on the plate. "That shit with the Skulls was bad enough. I don't want to go to war again."

"Nobody does. Except Vic."

"Did he tell you? I've asked him if I can retire."

Ellery raised his eyebrows. "What did he say?"

Brendan considered. "That he'd think about it."

"He'd think about it?"

"Yeah."

"Fair enough." Ellery's gaze wandered about the pub as he closed Brendan's newspaper, folded it, and tucked it under one arm. "Enjoy the rest of your lunch."

"Hey, that's my paper."

"You've finished with it, haven't you?"

"Yeah, sure." Brendan hesitated. "You reckon he'll let me go?"

Ellery made a dismissive gesture. "I would, if I were Vic."

"Yeah?"

"If your heart's not in it, your heart's not in it."

"Thanks mate. Could you put in a good word for me? In case he's having trouble making up his mind?"

"Sure." Ellery stood up. "Keep watching Abby. We'll let you know."

Brendan grimaced, shifted in his chair.

"What?" Ellery said. "Is there a problem?"

"Look, to be honest, I'd rather you gave the tailing job to Itchy."

Ellery pursed his mouth. "That's not up to you."

"Right, I was just putting it out there."

"As long as you're in the club," Ellery said, "you do what you're told."

"I know, yeah, no worries."

"Okay then. See you later, Danny Boy."

Distracted, rubbing at the scar on his knuckle, Brendan watched as Ellery walked the length of the bistro and pushed through the door marked Private. The door swung shut hard, juddering against the frame.

The barmaid, Rosie, approached the table, said, "Another beer?"

"Yeah," Brendan said. "Why not?"

"Hey, missed ya at the party the other night."

Brendan shrugged, made a non-committal grunt, kept staring at the door Ellery had gone through.

"Come to think of it," Rosie said, leaning onto the table to put her face into Brendan's line of sight, "I haven't seen ya at a get-together for yonks."

The legendary debauchery of the typical Overlords party included beer, speed, strippers, whores and brawls, the kinds of things that had once interested Brendan but not any more. So what? Rosie, however, was staring at him curiously. It made him wonder for the first time if they'd noticed how many times he was missing.

"I've been sick," he said.

"Oh, yeah?" Rosie stood up straight, put one hand on her hip. "It's been so long, you must be sick as a fucken dog. Get better soon, all right?"

Brendan had never been to an indoor play centre before.

The place was cavernous with an open, vaulted ceiling of metal struts and tin sheets. The front desk, kitchen and cafeteria took up about one-quarter of the floor space, while the rest contained play equipment on a giant scale – slides some eight metres high, jumping castles, rock-climbing walls, a huge fenced-off area with ride-on toys – and enough screaming, laughing, crying, yelling kids to give Brendan a headache, and he'd only been waiting fifteen minutes.

Two mothers sitting at a nearby table kept giving him dirty looks. Perhaps they were judging him on his yellowing facial bruises from that fight with the Jackals. Or maybe the mothers thought he was a pervert. After all, he was the only adult in the cafeteria without any trappings of parenthood: no newborn on his lap, no pram or pusher, no lunchbox with vegemite sandwiches or carrot sticks, no child-sized shoes scattered by his chair.

Aw, fuck 'em.

Checking his watch, he happened to again catch the disapproving eye of one of the mothers. Before he could decide how to respond, she sneered at him and turned her face. Ill at ease, he began tapping at his leg. For something to do, perhaps he could buy another espresso. As he turned to assess the length of the line at the counter, he spotted Nicole.

The blonde hair swinging loose around her shoulders and the lack of make-up made her look twenty years old. The moment she saw him, she broke into a grin. He stood up, clattering his chair, heart pounding.

Nicole trailed a boy in her wake.

Mostly, the boy was hidden behind her. Brendan glimpsed brown hair, a leg in blue jeans, an arm in a long-sleeved, stripy top.

"Hi," Nicole said, kissing Brendan on the cheek. "Find the place okay?"

Brendan nodded. The breath seized in his throat. Nicole reached back and steered the boy to the table. Brendan looked at his son for the first time in four years.

"Brendan, this is Max," Nicole said. "Max, this is... your daddy."

Max had green eyes, as green as Brendan's. His hair was messy, wavy, the colour of walnuts; his skin milky except for dark eyebrows, two hot flushes stamped on his cheeks, and a scabbed graze on his chin. The polo shirt hung from narrow shoulders, big ears poked out from his head. None of this felt real. Under Brendan's intense scrutiny, Max worked a shoe into the floor and pulled his mouth to one side as if chewing on his lip. Brendan felt the prickle of tears.

Max whispered to Nicole, "What do I call him?"

Daddy.

"Call him Brendan for now," she said. "Okay, Max, what do you say?"

"Huh?"

"Remember? What we talked about in the car."

"We talked about lots of things in the car."

"About, you know, the present. Remember?"

"Oh, yeah." Max stepped forward and solemnly put out his hand. "Thank you for the soccer ball thing."

"He means the Soccer Trainer," Nicole said.

Brendan took his son's hand. It was soft, warm, and small; a little sticky. A vision of Max as a baby came to mind. Hair in a tufted mohawk, cheeks full and fat. Did he recognise his own son? Could he see the baby he remembered in this boy? Brendan wasn't sure.

"I'm glad you liked the present," Brendan said, his voice a croak. "Your mum told me you like playing soccer."

"It's okay."

"I hear you're good at defence. Being goalic and all that?"

The boy lifted and dropped one shoulder. "Um, I guess."

Nicole pulled out one of the plastic chairs and said, "Let's sit down."

They did. Brendan saw that the two disapproving mothers on

the nearby table were now shooting polite, apologetic expressions at him.

"Can I go play?" Max said to Nicole.

"In a minute," she said.

Brendan couldn't take his eyes off him. "How old are you, Max?"

"Nearly seven."

"Do you like school?"

Max shrugged again. "It's okay."

Brendan said, "Your drawing was really great."

Children were squealing. Max looked away towards the slides.

"Max?" Nicole said.

"Huh?"

"Brendan said he liked your drawing."

"No, I love it," Brendan said. "It's the best drawing ever."

"Mum, can I go play now?"

"Don't you want to talk to Brendan a bit more first?"

"I want to go down that red slide, right on my guts this time."

"In a minute," Nicole said. "We've got all day."

"No, it's all right," Brendan said. Turning to Max, he added, "Off you go, give me a big Tarzan yell beforehand, okay?"

Max kicked off his sneakers, sprinted from the cafeteria and was swallowed up by the giant construct of play equipment. Brendan closed his eyes.

"Give it some time," Nicole said.

Brendan nodded. His stomach felt lodged inside his throat.

9

The secretary, old man Pinch, drove like a grandma: slowly, and with both hands on the steering wheel in the ten-to-two position. He even braked the car to a crawl before every green light. Annoyed, Brendan opened the passenger-side window and lit a smoke. It would be stupid to comment on the old man's crappy driving. These days, Pinch may be a frail pensioner slowly dying from prostate cancer, but he'd still knife you if he sensed any disrespect.

To make the journey worse, in the back seat were a couple of prospects; young men barely out of their teens, keyed up and anxious about their inaugural job for the Overlords. They kept cracking jokes and swearing, hitting at each other, laughing too loud.

"For fuck's sake, calm down," Brendan said, twisting around in his seat to glare at both of them. "Stop carrying on like little kids, all right?"

Chastened, the prospects nodded and shut up.

Pinch said, "Danny Boy, you'd have been just as nervous the first time out."

Brendan laughed. "Nah, not me, mate. I was Mr Too-Cool-for-School."

He had been seventeen years old, a dropout and dole bludger, full bearded in those days, muscular for his age and keen to throw his weight around, when a group of Overlords befriended him at the local pub one evening after witnessing the way he handled himself in a fistfight. The bikies always had money, and plenty of it. One of them, Johnny Smiles, liked to carry his cash in a fat roll secured with a rubber band. Lust for a cash roll of his own determined the course of Brendan's entire life.

His first job for the Overlords involved bashing a lawyer over a $20,000 cocaine debt. Brendan had never before hurt anyone in cold blood. The lawyer cried, begged, wet his pants. Brendan cried too, in fear and shock, but applied the crowbar as instructed, breaking the lawyer's forearms and shins while carefully avoiding every other body part so as not to kill the man by accident. When Brendan received his payment, he furled the notes and put a rubber band around them. The roll was pathetic, as skinny as his little finger, but it had meant a lot. With some of the money, he had bought a Sony Walkman cassette player, a state-of-the-art piece of equipment back in the eighties. That's how goddamned old he was now.

He blew a stream of smoke into the cabin of Pinch's car. His boyhood idol, Johnny Smiles, was dead some eight years: suicide, gunshot to the temple.

"Hey, Pinch," Brendan said. "Remember Johnny Smiles?"

"Yeah… top bloke."

"The bee's knees. You know, if it wasn't for him, I wouldn't have joined the Overlords. The poor bastard, too bad he offed himself."

"Hah." Pinch glanced around. "Sure about that?"

"What do you mean?"

"You're an old hand, Danny Boy. Connect the dots."

Brendan flicked his cigarette butt out the window. There had been rumours at the time that Johnny Smiles had turned informant, was about to tell the police everything he knew about the operations of the Overlords.

Brendan said, "So he didn't shoot himself? Someone else shot him?"

"I know nothing," Pinch said, and made a show of clamping his lips.

"So you're just guessing about Johnny Smiles, or what?"

"All right, let's say I'm guessing."

Brendan shook his head. "You're like the goddamned Sphinx sometimes."

"What?" came a voice from the rear of the car. "Were you talking to us?"

Brendan twisted in his seat and scowled.

The prospect, looking wounded, continued, "Shit, we can't hear a fucken thing over this music."

In reply, Pinch turned up the radio.

They reached their destination about forty minutes later. The business park contained offices and warehouses arranged along a cul-de-sac. Plenty of vehicles were coming and going at this lunchtime hour, which Brendan found reassuring: it was always best to hide in plain sight. Pinch tootled the car, looking this way and that, sucking on his bottom lip and frowning.

"Don't you know the address?" Brendan said.

"Stop fussing, Danny Boy."

Leaning between the front seats, the loudmouth prospect said, "Is everything okay?"

"Pull your head in," Brendan said. "Don't say another fucken word."

After driving up and down the cul-de-sac a few times, Pinch put the car into a factory driveway and sounded the horn. The roll-a-door opened. A man in overalls gestured *come on* with his whole arm. Pinch drove into the factory and the man closed the roll-a-door behind them.

They got out of the car. On the factory floor were three one-tonne Toyota Hi-Ace vans, the kind with no side windows. All three vehicles were white, clean, in immaculate condition.

The man in the overalls said, "Who are the drivers?"

Pinch pointed.

The man in overalls handed out keys to Brendan and the two prospects.

"Drive to the depot in Greensborough," Pinch said.

The loudmouth prospect, smirking, said, "That's it?"

"Yeah, shithead, that's it, so don't fuck it up," Pinch said. To Brendan he added, "See ya back at the Burley."

Brendan nodded. Pinch got into the car and waited.

"Stick to the speed limits," the man said to Brendan and the prospects. "Keep at least a kilometre distant from each other. Indicate when changing lanes, no texting, no chatting on mobile phones... are we clear? Don't draw attention to yourself."

Brendan sighed. He'd been pulling jobs like this back when the man in overalls had been wearing nappies.

They climbed into the vans. The man opened the roll-a-door. Pinch reversed out and left. The two prospects drove away next. Once Brendan got out on the road, he noticed that the van felt bogged into its shockers, as if loaded heavy. The rear-view mirror held stacks of brown cardboard boxes. Guns, drugs, stolen goods? He didn't know or care.

The day was cold and bright, the traffic reasonably light. He switched on the radio. An old Bad Company song belted out of the speakers. Brendan took it as an omen that everything was going to be all right. Blind runs like this were tricky. Luck had to be on your side. If police happened to pull you over, you had no idea what kind of charges you might be facing. Years ago, an Overlords driver with a flat tyre had ended up in prison after transit police, stopping to help, had discovered a body in the boot of his car.

At least, that was the story according to Johnny Smiles, who had always been a big one for the bullshit; maybe the body-in-the-boot story had been bullshit too.

Brendan lit a smoke.

Johnny Smiles...

It had been Johnny who had, indirectly, introduced Brendan to Nicole some twenty years ago. Johnny's cousin, a greasy-looking boy with long hair, was a bass guitarist in a mediocre band that played covers of popular rock songs. This one Saturday night, Johnny asked a few people to go along to a gig because, apparently, a talent scout would be in the crowd. Johnny hoped that an enthusiastic audience would help his cousin's rise to stardom. (Long story short: it didn't.) When Johnny Smiles asked a favour, it was an order.

The pub had a mixed crowd, ranging from rough-nuts like Brendan and his bikie mates through to yuppies in business suits. The band was terrible. Considering Johnny was always looking over at them, Brendan tried to act interested in the music. At the end of the first set, as the crowd mobbed the bar and the dance area thinned out, Brendan noticed a couple of girls near the stage.

Actually, he noticed only one.

She had masses of blonde curly hair – permed, he would later discover – piled on top of her head in a messy ponytail, and wore a tight black mini-skirt, heels and denim jacket. She glanced at him, looked away; glanced again. At twenty-seven, Brendan was clean-shaven, bigger than ever from regular gym workouts, a bruiser. He sucked on his beer stubby and watched her. She talked to her friend, preening now, aware of his admiration.

The band started the next set, their renditions no better. Nonetheless, drunken patrons again crammed the dance floor. Brendan lost sight of the girl. A few songs later, he saw her. She was dancing, wriggling her hips, backing up slowly but surely through the crowd, looking around at him every once in a while, until he finally realised that she was *aiming* for him.

Unbelievable.

Then he watched her nudge through his group of bikie mates. They fell back, laughing and spluttering at her audacity, jeering at Brendan, crowing. When she was close enough, she asked him to dance.

Brendan had never danced a single step in his life.

His mates shoved at him, taunting and mocking. The girl ignored them all. She saw Brendan and nobody else. Her skin was so clear, so smooth, the whites of her eyes so bright. He wanted to kiss her.

"Well?" she yelled over the music. "Are you gonna dance with me or what?"

And he danced. Tried his best to find the beat in the music, shifted his feet one-two, one-two, lifting his arms clumsily. He felt as graceful as Frankenstein's monster, but so what, the girl's radiant smile encouraged him, tugged at the nerves in his belly. Meanwhile, the blokes howled with laughter. When Brodie dangled an unwrapped condom in the girl's face, Brendan shoved him with enough force to bounce him off the bar.

Brendan kept dancing.

The girl did too.

They danced together for the next song, and the next, the one after that. At the break, he grabbed her hand and led her outside so they could hear each other talk.

"I'm Nicole," she said.

"Brendan. Can I get your phone number?"

She shook her head. "No, give me yours."

"What if you don't ring me?"

"Promise, I'll ring tomorrow night at nine-thirty, okay? On the dot."

He told her his number. She wrote it down on the back of her hand. The next night, waiting for her scheduled call, he found that he couldn't relax. When the phone sounded, he sprinted down the hall, shouting at his flatmates to leave it, just fucken *leave it*.

Their date the following Thursday was supposed to be for dinner. As it turned out, they got drunk at a bar instead. Going back to her place, he intended to kiss her chastely and leave, but she unzipped him. He stepped back.

"I should go," he said.

Nicole appeared shocked, insulted. "Why? Don't you want me?"

"Shit, more than anything."

"Then what's wrong?"

"I don't want to treat you like a slut."

"A slut?"

Nicole laughed, making him blush. Her kiss shot an electric jolt through him.

Drawing away, he said, "Wait a second. I'm trying to do the right thing here."

"Aw, don't worry." She reached inside his jeans, took him in her hand. "I'll still respect you in the morning."

Their first night together had been amazing, the chemistry a shock to them both; a revelation. Sex brought them back together after every breakup. No other woman could do it for him like Nicole, and he suspected that it was the same for her with other men.

They were on-again off-again for about ten years.

One night when they were on-again, she told him that she wanted to have his baby. In reply, he proposed to her. No, to be honest, he didn't actually propose, not quite. He said, as a hypothetical, "Wouldn't you want to get married first?"

She tipped her head to one side, as if considering.

"Yeah, all right, I'll marry you," she said, acting casual, as if it were no big deal. Then squealing, she flung her arms about his neck and kissed him until he felt breathless. He was about to say, *hey, that's not what I meant*, until he realised that yes, deep down it was exactly what he meant.

Their wedding took place at the Registry Office in the city of Melbourne. As witnesses, they had his mate Brodie and Nicole's best friend, both of whom had been at the pub where he and Nicole had met all those years ago. The ceremony lasted a few minutes. Afterwards, they drank the afternoon away at a nearby bar. Nicole was radiant, the happiest he'd ever seen her. Every time she looked at him, he could see the love in her eyes. That was nine years ago. Another time, almost another world. Now, it was like remembering somebody else's life.

Brendan lit a cigarette, changed lanes in the Toyota Hi-Ace.

Whisky and pills had ruined his marriage. No, strictly speaking, the catalyst had been the event that had driven him to whisky and pills in the first place. The killing.

Vic had ordered him to kill someone.

A bikie from a rival club, a bloke named Waldo.

Brendan hadn't wanted to do it. But you can't refuse your president. So Brendan had done what he was told and then... then couldn't get the images out of his head, couldn't look Nicole in the face. Whisky helped. But he needed pills to counteract the hangovers, the depression. Soon, he needed the pills just to get out of bed in the morning, and whisky to come down from the tooth-grinding highs. By the time it dawned on him that he had a problem, Nicole was already pregnant with Max, and Brendan felt too dependent on pills and whisky to ever contemplate sobriety.

He braked the Hi-Ace at a red light. The cardboard boxes drew his gaze to the rear-view mirror. He flipped his cigarette butt through the open window. If he hadn't become an Overlord, then what? Maybe a tradesman. A plumber, a carpenter, a brick layer. Or, more likely, something that didn't require qualifications like a factory worker, painter, brickie's labourer, truck driver. A real job nonetheless, where he paid taxes, got annual leave, had self-respect. He should have tried a little harder back in the day, should have disciplined himself a little more instead of taking the easy way, the fast way, the wrong way. But who was that smart at seventeen years of age? Not him, that's for sure. Not when a fat roll of money had seemed the answer to everything.

The light turned green. Brendan stamped his foot on the accelerator. *Aw, just get to the goddamned depot in Greensborough, and stop raking over the past.* Besides, things were looking better for him these days. He'd messed up his life, but was fixing things now. Wasn't he?

Take it easy. Watch the road and take it easy.

10

O n Thursday, Brendan made his collections. At the tattoo parlour in Bayswater, the owner, Tina, her arm in a cast, handed over the money without speaking or meeting his eye. She looked exhausted, as if she hadn't eaten or slept. He felt bad for her. Then again, Brendan had his own worries.

Last night, in retaliation for the bullets that Itchy had fired into the left leg of both Farid and Talal, the Golden Jackals had firebombed an Overlords satellite clubhouse, a place in Lancefield. The molotov cocktail had burnt the paint on the front door, the eaves, damaged nothing else. A poor showing, Vic had said, gloating: *They should've chucked the fucker through a window.*

It was starting again; Vic was pulling the club into yet another pointless, bloody war. How many other members were sick and tired of Vic's combative leadership? Brendan knew for a fact that Ellery didn't want to fight the Jackals. Now *there* was a man who would make a damn good president.

If only Vic were out of the way.

"It's only dinner, for Christ's sake," Nicole said, "what's the big deal?"

Two minutes into her visit and they were fighting already.

Brendan got up from the couch, opened the single window in his lounge room, and lit a cigarette. The afternoon was overcast and mild. Shoppers were going about their business on the footpaths below. Cars whisked back and forth. Faintly through the floor came the sound of the butcher, singing, thumping a meat-axe into a chopping board.

"I wouldn't feel comfortable," Brendan said at last.

"Why not?"

"Your mum hates my guts."

"So?"

"So she'd probably try to poison me."

"Christ, I told you already, I'm going to be doing the cooking, not her." With an exasperated sigh, Nicole added, "All right, fine, let's make it Monday. Every Monday night, the old bird plays cards at a friend's house and doesn't come home 'til midnight. You, me and Max for a home-cooked meal, what's wrong with that?"

Nicole walked over, grabbed him by the jaw, and forced him to look at her.

After a few seconds of eye contact, they both started to grin.

"Okay," he said, laughing, pushing away her hand. "What's on the menu?"

"I don't know. Steak and chips, I haven't thought that far ahead."

"Does Max know?"

Nicole smiled. "It was his idea."

For a moment, the breath lodged in Brendan's chest. "Max wants me to come over for tea?"

"You made a big impression on him at the play centre."

"But we barely spoke. He was too busy playing." Brendan gazed out the window, stared at the traffic. "It must be the Soccer Trainer."

"No," she said, moving closer. "It's you."

She leaned against him, rested her cheek against his chest. A minute slid by. He took a final drag of his smoke and crushed the butt in the ashtray.

"Hey," he said. "I got you something."

Nicole drew back and looked up at him. "A present?"

He pointed at a brown paper bag on the kitchen bench.

"For me?" she said.

"Go find out."

She went over, smiled at him uncertainly, and then looked inside the bag. Her smile fell away. Reaching into the bag, she pulled out the banded sheaves of money and stared at them, confused, as if she didn't recognise them.

"Five grand," Brendan said.

"Five grand?"

"For child support. I figure I must owe you about sixty. It's a down payment."

She didn't say anything. Brendan went over and put an arm around her.

"What am I going to do with all of this?" she whispered.

"Anything you like." He kissed her forehead. "I'll have more next week."

She pushed away from him. "What's going on?"

"Huh?"

"You have to tell me," she said. "I've got a right to know."

The phone rang. Lifting a finger to say *hang on a second*, Brendan moved to the kitchen wall and grabbed the handset.

"Yeah?" he said.

"It's Ellery."

"What's up?"

"Get to the Burley now."

The line went dead. Brendan turned to Nicole. She looked

anxious, fearful, the wide cast of her eyes breaking his heart in a myriad of different ways.

Brendan walked into the Burley. The bistro was almost deserted a couple of hours past the close of lunchtime service. At a table near the bar sat Ellery and Itchy, both looking sombre. Ellery stood up at Brendan's approach.

"G'day," Brendan said. "Something wrong?"

In reply, Ellery gestured with his thumb for Brendan to follow. With a glance at Itchy, who remained seated, Brendan trailed Ellery through the door marked Private and along the hallway. Instead of continuing to the boardroom, however, Ellery stopped outside a door marked Manager, which was Vic's office. Ellery rapped a knuckle.

"Come in," Vic called.

They went inside. Vic was sitting at his desk.

Ellery shut the door behind them. Brendan hadn't stepped foot in Vic's office for years. The decor hadn't changed all that much, as far as Brendan could remember. One corner still held a bar fridge. The back wall still had the painting of a flaming skeleton riding a motorbike, a Southern Cross flag, a poster of Ned Kelly, a Jack Daniels mirror. But the wall opposite Vic's desk was now a memorial to his dead nephew, Drago, killed in the drive-by shooting that had sparked the Overlords war with the Skulls some eight years ago.

"Recognise him?" Vic said, pointing at the wall of photographs.

"Yeah, it's Drago."

Vic got up from his desk, stood next to Brendan, and said, "He was a good looking boy, don't you reckon?"

"Yeah, sure."

"See this one here? He liked boxing."

Brendan looked over the photographs. The collection included framed newspaper articles of Drago's murder, the subsequent war. *A killer is killed* read one headline. *Overlords vs. Skulls* read another. *Bikie showdown, police turn blind eye.*

"Only twenty years old." Vic touched a photograph. "See this?"

Brendan leaned in. The small colour snapshot showed a concrete floor spattered in blood. "Gruesome," he said.

"Gruesome?" Vic shoved at him. "That's my nephew's blood."

"No, I mean that a picture like that must upset you."

"It's supposed to upset me, arsehole. That's how I never forget him."

Ellery pulled out a couple of chairs, saying, "Come on… let's start the meeting."

They all sat down. Vic ran both hands through his hair, taking a few seconds to get composed. Brendan and Ellery waited in respectful silence.

Then Vic smiled. "The two grand you owe me. Consider it repaid in full."

"Aw, thanks," Brendan said. "From the money I took off Farid, right?"

"Wrong. For services yet to be rendered," Vic continued. "Take care of Abdullah Hanoush."

Brendan couldn't find his voice. Finally, he said, "What?"

Vic said, "Do it this weekend."

"You mean… kill him?" Brendan said. "You want me to kill Abby?"

"Vic wants to push back against the Jackals," Ellery said. "The decision's made, there's no sense in dithering."

Their faces were cold, set. Brendan clasped his hands together, squeezing them tightly, cracking the knuckles. "How come you don't want Itchy to do it?"

"Because I want you to do it," Vic said.

"Get the gun off Itchy before you leave," Ellery said.

"Shoot Abby in the head," Vic said. "The full clip, I want that fucker looking like mincemeat. Beat him too, the more injuries the better. Take a tyre lever with you. Hop into him once he's cactus, really go to town on the prick. This has to be a message they'll never forget, okay?"

"Listen, Danny Boy, the gun is clean."

"But don't take chances. Chuck it away as soon as you're done."

"We suggest you break it down, drop the pieces in dumpsters in different suburbs. Look out for CCTV cameras. Put each part in a plastic bag full of rubbish, so if you're seen on video, it looks like you're getting rid of household waste. Now this is important… we only want Abby done at this stage."

"But if some cocksucker gets in your way, shoot them too."

"Try to get him when he's alone. The Jackals will realise it's us anyway, but why give them confirmation through witnesses?"

"Any witnesses though, if they're Jackals, go ahead and shoot the fuckers."

"Do you have questions?"

They fell silent at last, staring at him, waiting for his response. Brendan's mouth felt dry. He licked his lips. Showing his palms, he wanted to say, *wait a second, just hold on a goddamned second*, but his throat had closed over.

"Well?" Vic said, face darkening.

Brendan shook his head.

Vic leaned across the desk. "You're gonna turn down your president?"

Ellery sighed. "Don't refuse the job, Danny Boy."

"I don't understand," Brendan whispered, "why the… how come you…"

"This bullshit about retiring," Vic said. "Are you with us? Then prove it. All right, the meeting is over, get out of here."

Brendan couldn't move. Vic kicked at him under the desk. Brendan scrambled to his feet. Glancing at Ellery, he saw something like compassion or regret in the man's face, as if he were trying to say, *if it were up to me, Danny Boy, I'd let you retire.* What had Ellery said about that just the other day?

If your heart's not in it, your heart's not in it.

If only Vic could see things the same way.

"What the fuck are you waiting for?" Vic yelled.

Brendan nodded, left the room, closed the door behind him. Racing along the hallway, pushing through the door, heart pounding, he was halfway across the bistro when he remembered the gun. He turned around.

Itchy was glaring at him from the table near the bar.

Brendan walked over, sat down opposite Itchy. The man's eyes were as cold and blue as ice chips. Fleetingly, Brendan imagined the pleasure Itchy would have taken in breaking the tattooist's arm. No, it didn't bear thinking about.

"I need the gun," Brendan said.

Itchy reached into his jacket, pulled out a Beretta 9mm, and placed it on the table. Brendan transferred it to the pocket of his own jacket.

"Thanks," he said, and stood up.

"You better do a good job," Itchy said. "Understand?"

"Huh? Yeah, sure."

"No, Danny Boy." Itchy raised his ginger eyebrows. "Do you understand?"

Without answering, Brendan fled the bistro, shoving through the double doors and hurrying across the veranda and down the steps to the car park, the frigid air burning his lungs. Overhead, cockatoos wheeled and screeched. Clouds hunkered low as if a storm was brewing.

11

Brendan spent that Saturday drunk.

On Sunday morning, hungover and queasy, he tailed Abby's ute along side streets, a major road, and then into the car park of a huge Bunnings warehouse. Easing into a space near the single entrance, Brendan killed the Holden's engine and waited.

Half a minute later, Abby walked the pedestrian crossing to the entrance. Abby wore tracksuit pants and a long-sleeved top, unmistakeable on account of his rangy physique, the runner's spring in his step. He went inside.

Brendan exhaled. The Beretta dug into his chest. He took the gun from his jacket and put it on the passenger seat. The gun looked very big. After a moment, he opened the glove box and stuffed it inside. The radio station was mewling a sugary tune. Brendan changed the station. Advert, advert, advert; a song he couldn't stand; advert, advert; back to the sugary tune; advert. He snapped off the radio.

Time passed.

People were streaming in and out of the hardware store. What could they possibly be buying in there? Recently, Brendan had read that admissions to Australian casualty departments were through the roof thanks to weekend do-it-yourself enthusiasts who kept cutting off their hands and whatnot in garage accidents. He'd never been one for making things. Yes, he could change a fuse or tap washer, replace a broken roof tile, but building anything from scratch? Forget it.

Cracking the window, his gaze fixed on the Bunnings open door, he lit another cigarette. The smoke made him feel ill. He'd smoked so much these past couple of days he could hardly breathe, his lungs wheezing in protest. Coughing, head pounding, he dragged on the cigarette anyway. It was surreal but he had to shoot Abby. Just like he'd had to shoot Waldo. Despite years of careful mental discipline, Brendan's mind flew back to the driveway of Waldo's suburban house.

...and to the Land Rover parked there, jittering and rumbling, its diesel engine as loud as a tractor. Waldo had just reversed the Land Rover out of the garage and got out, was pulling down the garage door, twisting the handle to close it. The sergeant-at-arms for the Skulls was a chunky man, bald, wearing jeans and a singlet, his neck and shoulders covered in blue tattoos. Brendan ran up the driveway behind him, silent on crepe-soled shoes, arm extended, gun in hand, gawping at the back of Waldo's bald head...

...*do it*, Brendan told himself, *do it, do it*...

...and then he froze. The gun shook.

Shit, oh shit; please don't turn around.

Waldo was still looking down, unaware, messing with the key-ring as if searching for the right key to lock the garage door, his skull a fragile egg. Precious seconds passed. Brendan, steeling himself, grimacing, turned his face...

...pulled the trigger and...

...blood hit the garage door in a loud, messy spray...

...and Waldo fell, as thoroughly and completely as wet cement off a trowel. Brendan sprinted back to the car and threw himself inside. Itchy stamped the accelerator and the car fishtailed away. And that was supposed to be that.

Except the killing had kept Brendan awake at night.

The manner in which Waldo had dropped to the driveway, boneless, had given Brendan the kind of shivers that only whisky could soothe. Nicole had woken him from countless bad dreams: Waldo swivelling his broken head on top of his broken neck, grinning wildly, crazily; spitting gouts of blood through ruined teeth. At the time, pregnant with Max, Nicole had asked repeatedly, "Why can't you tell me what's wrong?" *Because you'd leave me.* His stoicism had meant nothing in the end. Nicole had left him anyway for many different reasons, all of them because he hadn't been able to put the killing behind him.

Each customer exiting out of Bunnings triggered a wave of adrenaline through Brendan's guts. He switched the car radio back on. The song happened to be an old Cold Chisel number, one of his favourites. He turned up the volume. For a time, he tapped his fingertips on the steering wheel, keeping time with the song. Then Abby appeared.

Brendan sat bolt upright.

Abby was pushing a trolley that barely held a flat cardboard box as big as a table. Looking both ways for cars, Abby steered the trolley over the pedestrian crossing. As the box passed almost alongside, Brendan saw its huge label: a photograph of a blocky construction in blue and pink plastic, the words *Heaps-A-Fun Cubby House* in fat, cheery letters.

Brendan snapped off the radio, twisted the key in the ignition.

Knowing the way to Abby's house allowed him to keep a long tail. As the garage door closed behind Abby's ute, Brendan drove past at speed.

He would return at nightfall to do the job.

"Hello?"

"Hey, you," Brendan said, tightening his grip on the handset.

"Oh, hey yourself." Nicole's voice sounded tinny, as if the phone connection spanned the world instead of a dozen suburbs.

"I was worried your mum would answer," he said.

"Then you should've called my mobile."

"I suppose," he said. "How're you doing?"

"Good. What about you?"

Leaning against his kitchen bench, he couldn't think of how to answer.

Nicole said, "Baby?"

"I'm here."

"What's going on?"

"Nothing," he said. "You want me to bring something tomorrow night for tea?"

"Don't bring anything. I'm making shepherd's pie. Is that still your favourite?"

"Anything you make is my favourite."

"I was going to make lasagne."

"That's my favourite too."

After a time, she said, "Are you okay?"

"Yeah."

"You want me to come over?"

"No." Tears prickled hot in his eyes. "Let me ask you something."

"Okay."

"Why do you love me?"

She actually laughed. "What kind of dumb question is that?"

"I need to know."

Finally, she said, "I dunno, I just do."

Outside his flat window, the sun was setting. He would have to get going. The gun felt heavy in his jacket pocket. Brendan closed his eyes.

Nicole said, "Are you still there?"

"Yeah," he said. "I'll see you tomorrow."

Then he hung up.

12

The backyard ran in a long, narrow rectangle from the kitchen door. There was evidence of some half-hearted landscaping – a hedgerow along the fence, a rockery, a fish pond – but it looked like the garden had been left to the elements for a long time. Bushes were shapeless, gangly and overgrown. The lawn was a patchwork of dirt and weeds, of holes dug by the dog.

"You're a naughty boy, aren't you?" Brendan whispered, rubbing at the dog's fluffy ears. "Oh yes, you are. Look at what you've done to the grass."

The dog panted with its tongue hanging out. In the dim light, its eyes shone wet like brown puddles. Brendan pulled the dog closer and began stroking it from head to tail. Was it a Shih Tzu, a Maltese terrier or some kind of cross? He didn't know his dog breeds. Whatever it was, no wonder Abby had chosen this particular pet for his children. Perhaps Max might like to have a friendly little dog like this one. Brendan decided to ask Nicole about it tomorrow.

First, he just had to get through tonight.

He was sitting on the concreted edge of the fish pond. The deep shadows cast by the Japanese maple and surrounding plants kept him well hidden. From his vantage point, he watched the brightly-lit kitchen. Every now and then, Abby or his black-haired, sloe eyed wife would pass by the window, ferrying children or bowls of food.

Abby and his wife must socialise a lot. The kitchen door opened directly onto a paved and roofed entertainment area. The cast-metal table had twelve chairs. The barbecue was one of those giant stainless steel ones on rollers, the expensive kind that replicates a full stovetop. The biggest giveaway, however, was the immaculate condition of the entertainment area in contrast to the rest of the yard. They must have family get-togethers out here all the time. Christmas, Easter, birthdays; every event would be a lavish affair with Abby steering the barbecue, his wife topping up the drinks, platters filling the table, lots of talking and laughing, kids running around.

Brendan took a breath, exhaled noisily. The dog cocked its head at him. He grabbed the dog and hugged it close.

"Who's a good boy?" he whispered at its ear. "Hey? You're a good boy."

Beyond the pool of light thrown by the kitchen window sat a wooden kennel, and by the kennel, a water bowl and an empty food dish.

Brendan checked his watch. It was coming up to seven p.m.

"Getting hungry, boy?" he whispered. "Is it nearly tea-time?"

Whining, the dog struggled out of Brendan's arms and scampered away down the length of the yard, disappearing into the murk. Brendan straightened out his legs. He'd been waiting in Abby's backyard for some ninety minutes by now, had hopped the fence soon after nightfall. The cold was hurting his joints. He blew into his cupped hands. Too bad he'd left his gloves in the car, but every time he thought about going back to get them, he decided against it, worried that he would miss his chance.

Abby's wife crossed the kitchen window, a child in her arms. Behind her followed Abby, grinning, holding the other child while its chubby hands pulled at his ears. They moved past the window and out of sight. After a brief time, Brendan heard the faint sound of running water. The bathroom must be nearby. He checked his watch: a few minutes after seven. They were drawing a bath for their children.

He sat up, leaned over, tried to work the kinks out of his back.

A noise that he couldn't identify made him panic. He snatched for the Beretta in his jacket pocket. It was only the dog, ambling up the dirt pathway, emerging from the dark with a jaunty step and its tongue lolling out. It paused to sniff at him.

"Hey there, little mate," Brendan whispered. "What you been doing out there? Digging more holes?"

The snap of a latch threw Brendan's heart into his throat. The dog took off at a trot. A door creaked. Slipping, scrambling, Brendan got up.

Abby was shuffling across the patio towards the kennel, an open tin in one hand, a spoon in the other. He wore the same grey tracksuit pants as yesterday, moccasins, no socks, a wide-necked t-shirt. Unshaven, he looked tired, ready to put his feet up in front of the TV. The kitchen door closed on its pneumatic hinge. The dog leapt at him, yapping.

"Here you go, Snowball," Abby said, "chicken, rice and vegetables this time."

Abby emptied the tin into the food bowl. Snowball began to eat.

Brendan emerged from the shadows, gun in hand.

Abby froze. Brendan took another step into the light and extended his arm, pointing the gun. Abby dropped the tin and spoon.

"You know what this is about?" Brendan said.

Abby tensed, but his facial expression remained closed, unreadable. "It's Danny Boy, right? The Irishman?"

"Well, you know, for what it's worth, I was born here. My parents are Irish."

The noise of running water kept on. The bath wasn't yet full. The murmur of voices sounded. Abby glanced behind him towards the house.

"Don't worry about them," Brendan said. "They'll be all right."

"Bullshit. Vic wants to go after civilians now."

"Who told you that?"

Abby didn't reply.

Brendan said, "Have you been talking with an Overlord?"

"Fuck you."

"Who have you been talking to?"

"Listen up. If you hurt my family, this shit will come back on you a hundred-fold. You know that, don't you? On you and everyone you love."

"I'm not after your wife and kids."

"Just me?"

"That's right. Just you."

The dog ate with gusto, a wet, sloppy noise. Brendan tightened his finger on the trigger, hesitated, the metal of the gun warm under his cold and shivering hand, warm from being held against his body for so long. He wondered about the cubby house that Abby had bought today. It was probably hidden in the garage, a present for the twins' upcoming second birthday.

The dog finished its meal with a loud gulp, and wandered over towards Brendan, licking its jaws.

"Snowball, no," Abby hissed. "Come here."

"You think I'd shoot a dog?"

Snowball paused, looked from one man to the other. Then it trotted out of the light towards the darkness at the other end of the yard. Both men watched it go.

Abby's mouth tightened into a straight line. "Fuck, Danny Boy, if you're gonna do it, come on, fucking-well do it."

Brendan raised the gun. His hand shook.

The sound of running bathwater ceased. Both men reacted, their wide eyes mirrored in each other's faces. Then the singing started. The wife sang first, the babbling voices of the children joining in here and there. Brendan recognised the theme from Spongebob Squarepants straight away. He hadn't heard it in ages, not since Max was a toddler, not since the three of them had been a family.

"Don't hurt them," Abby said.

"I won't."

"Swear on it."

"I swear."

Brendan held the gun at arm's length. Abby gritted his teeth, braced. The singing kept on and on. Brendan's finger stuttered against the trigger.

He couldn't do it. Not now, not ever.

He lowered the gun.

For a moment, the men stared at each other in disbelief. And then, stuffing the gun into his jacket pocket, Brendan turned and fled. Get away, he had to *get away*. He vaulted the fence, fell, ran through the front yard to the footpath and staggered to the car, his heart knocking against his ribs hard enough to break them.

13

Sleep wouldn't come. No surprise there.

Brendan gave up at around one a.m. and spent the rest of the night in front of the TV, chain-smoking and drinking beer. For hours, he flipped between old movies, Major League baseball replays from the US, demonstrations of non-stick saucepans, and religious programs full of hallelujah. Around sunrise, he felt tired enough to lie down.

A hammering on his door woke him up.

He rolled out of bed, rubbed at the cricks in his neck. His mouth tasted sour, and the clock showed it was just after eleven in the morning. The place was as cold as a meat locker; he needed to switch on the heater.

Standing next to the door, he said, "Who is it?"

"Open up, Danny Boy."

He recognised Ellery's voice and turned the lock. The door shoved open with great force, staggering him. Itchy was suddenly in his face.

"What the fuck?" Brendan said.

"Let's everybody calm down," Ellery said, closing the door. "Itchy... rustle up some coffee. Danny Boy, I assume you've got a jar of instant somewhere in your pantry?"

"Sure," Brendan mumbled. "Knock yourselves out."

He retreated to his bedroom to grab a T-shirt to put on over his shorts. When he turned around, Ellery was leaning in the doorway with folded arms. Brendan froze for a second. Then he reached down to the bedside table and grabbed his watch.

"You know what I think is strange?" Ellery said.

"What?" Brendan said, putting on his watch.

"The fact you don't have a mobile phone. You're the only person I know who doesn't own one." Ellery made a soft harrumphing sound, as if to clear his throat. "Danny Boy, we've been trying to call you all morning."

"My landline's off the hook."

"And why's that?"

"I wanted a sleep-in."

The kettle boiled and subsided. Brendan brushed past Ellery and headed to the bathroom. When Ellery followed, Brendan put a hand to the man's chest. Incredulous, Ellery looked down at it as if he couldn't believe his eyes.

Hastily retracting his hand, Brendan said, "Look, I just need a piss."

"Yes, of course," Ellery said. "Take your time."

Brendan shut the door. The lock was a simple one, easily broken, a skinny bolt pushed into a latch, but he engaged it anyway. This was the first time that Ellery and Itchy had ever been here. After flushing the toilet, Brendan washed his face and hands, ran a comb through his hair. In the mirror, he looked pale and frightened.

He came out of the bathroom. Ellery was sitting on the couch. Brendan went to the window, lit a cigarette, switched on the heater, and opened the blind. The morning was overcast. Itchy walked into the lounge room holding three mugs in one fist. He gave a mug to Ellery and another to Brendan. Each coffee was black. Itchy sat on the couch next to Ellery and slurped at the coffee. As Brendan sipped at the bitter, scalding liquid, he thought about the Beretta 9mm in his jacket that was right now hanging on the back of the single kitchen chair.

"So?" Ellery said.

"So," Brendan replied. "To what do I owe the honour?"

Ellery's half-smile didn't have any mirth in it. "Ah, you're a card, Danny Boy. Is this actually where you live?"

"Yeah."

"I expected something more... upmarket."

"You mean like me?" Brendan said, attempting a joke.

Ellery and Itchy didn't laugh.

Taking a long, hard drag on his smoke, Brendan said, "I know why you're here. You want to know about Abby."

Ellery nodded and spread his hands, as if to say, *enlighten us.*

Brendan hadn't thought this far ahead. Finally, he said, "I tried."

"You tried?" Ellery said. "What does that mean?"

"Things didn't work out."

"Abdullah Hanoush is still alive?"

"Like I said, I tried."

"Tried in what way?"

Brendan smoked the cigarette down to the filter and crushed it against the ashtray. "I followed him all Saturday and Sunday, but he kept going to public places."

"Vic wanted it done on the weekend. Today is Monday."

"Yeah, I know, but I couldn't get a clean shot."

Ellery glanced at Itchy. As if uninterested, Itchy just gulped at coffee.

"Where's the gun we gave you?" Ellery said. "Is it here?"

Brendan hesitated. "No."

"All right," Ellery said. "Until Abdullah Hanoush is done, you'll take your orders from Itchy or me by phone or in person. Don't come to the Burley for now."

"Huh? I can't come to the clubhouse?"

"No."

"What?" Brendan said. "That's fucked. Says who?"

"Says Vic."

Brendan felt a surge of alarm. "I've been an Overlord for thirty fucken years, almost since the beginning, since before Vic had even heard of the club."

Ellery shrugged. "Vic is getting paranoid in his old age. Don't worry about it."

"He thinks I'm a threat?"

"You know how he is."

"Well, shit, do you think I'm a threat?"

"Danny Boy," Ellery said, "it doesn't matter a jot what I think."

Ellery stood up. Itchy did too. They walked to the kitchen and put their coffee mugs on the bench. Brendan followed. Itchy opened the door. Cold air fanned into the flat. Itchy's red Clubsport was parked in the laneway, blocking the thoroughfare for every tenant. Once over the threshold, Ellery turned and clapped a hand on Brendan's shoulder, gazing at him intently, soberly, as if he would never lay eyes on him again. This raised the hair on Brendan's neck.

"Goodbye," Ellery said.

"Yeah sure, okay," Brendan said as they left. "See you later."

"Not if I see you first," Itchy called.

Brendan slammed the door and locked it. Had they found the gun? Caught him in a lie? They'd had time to do a quick search of the flat while he was getting dressed, taking a piss. Hurrying across the kitchen, he grabbed his jacket from the chair and fumbled at its inner pocket. His fingers closed around the Beretta.

He breathed out, sat heavily in the chair. Then it occurred to him that perhaps they had found the gun but decided not to take it or mention it. Either way, he couldn't stall forever. He'd have to confess that he hadn't been able to kill Abby. That he could never kill him. Vic would see the refusal as a betrayal.

But how would Vic react?

And for that matter, how would Abby and the Golden Jackals react to the botched assassination attempt? No doubt they would want revenge on Vic for ordering the hit. But would they feel grateful towards Brendan for his last-minute show of compassion? Or would they come after him anyway?

Sweating despite the chill, Brendan lit a cigarette and tried to think it through, tried to figure out what he should do next.

14

Darkness was falling. Brendan parked in front of his ex-mother-in-law's house, and cut the engine. The last time he'd been here was four years ago, Christmas Day, back when he and Nicole were playing out the final miserable weeks of their marriage. Drunk by lunchtime, Brendan had dropped into a banana lounge and tipped it over, spilling himself onto the concrete patio. His mother-in-law had laughed. Nicole and Max had known better. Infuriated, Brendan had snatched up the banana lounge and hurled it at the garden shed with enough force to buckle the galvanised steel walls. And what had his mother-in-law called him during the ensuing argument? *A rotten, stinking, no-good son-of-a-bitch.*

Brendan winced at the memory. He gathered up the bag of gifts from the passenger seat, exited the car, and walked down the driveway. The cream brick bungalow looked welcoming with its soft, warm glow around the curtained windows. He rang the doorbell. As footsteps approached, a tremor of anxiety flittered through his guts. *Relax. You can do this.*

Nicole opened the door and smiled. "Six o'clock, right on time." She got up on tip-toes to kiss him.

"Let me check," he said. "When's your mum coming home?"

"Midnight... later if she's winning at poker. It's okay. Come on in."

The entrance hall was exactly as he remembered, decked out

89

in velour wallpaper and fussy, baroque mirrors. Nicole closed the door.

"The shepherd's pie smells great," he said, following her into the lounge room.

"It's the same recipe. Max, you remember Brendan?"

Max was sitting in one of the recliner armchairs, his feet dangling, wet hair combed precisely across his scalp, the collared shirt looking as if it were prickling at him. Brendan's heart gave a messy little jangle.

"Hey there," Brendan said. "How's it going?"

"Okay. What's in the bag?"

"Presents."

The boy's face lit up as he leapt from the chair. "For me too?"

"Yeah, of course." Brendan reached into the bag, handed over a box and continued, "You like chocolate, right?"

"Sure, who doesn't?"

"And these are for soccer."

"What are they?" Max said, grabbing hold of the package.

"Socks."

Max screwed up his face. "Socks?"

"Long ones so you don't lose your shin pads."

"But they're yellow."

"Max," Nicole said in a cautioning voice.

"They're Socceroo socks," Brendan continued, "like the ones the players wear. Open them up. They've got the green symbol on the sides."

The boy shrugged. "I don't know what a Socceroo is."

Nicole said, "He plays soccer, but he doesn't really follow it."

"Oh," Brendan said. "But chocolate is still pretty good, right?"

Max wandered back to the recliner, put the chocolate and socks on the coffee table and sat down, regarding Brendan with sombre eyes.

"What do you say?" Nicole said.

"Thank you," Max intoned.

"Come into the kitchen," she said to Brendan. "I'll get you a drink."

She poured his beer. He handed her the bag. Looking inside, she blanched.

"What?" he said.

"Nothing."

"That's almost two grand in there."

She put the bag on the kitchen bench. "Where are you getting the money?"

"From work."

"Work?" She shook her head. "That's what you're calling it these days?"

"Yeah. If you don't want the money, throw it back at me and I'll go."

She grabbed at his chin and angled his face so that he had to look at her. After a moment, they both started smiling.

"Thanks for the presents," she said.

"That you both hate."

"Look, this is new for me and Max, okay?" she whispered. "And for you as well. Give it time."

He leant down and kissed her, gently.

She broke away. "I need a few minutes to serve up dinner. Go chat with Max."

The boy was still sitting in the recliner, looking bored.

Brendan sat opposite him on the coffee table and said, "You know what I should get you next?"

"Matching yellow undies?"

Brendan laughed. Blushing, Max grinned. So Brendan's son had a sense of humour. It felt good, sharing this moment together. Then Brendan thought about the countless moments they had

91

missed already, moments they could never get back, and the good feeling soured.

"No, a puppy," Brendan continued, "I should get you a little dog that could be your best mate. How would that be?"

"Nana hates dogs."

"Yeah? How come?"

"She reckons they poop everywhere."

"Maybe Nana would let you have a dog if you promised to train it right."

Max rolled his eyes. "You don't know Nana."

Oh, yes I do. Instead, Brendan said, "Maybe you and your mum could live somewhere else."

"We've got nowhere else to go."

Brendan paused. "Maybe you could live with someone who likes dogs."

"I don't know anybody."

"Well, I like dogs."

Max didn't seem to hear. "My best friend Jayden has a dog but it barks too much. Jayden's dad reckons that he's gonna get the barker in its throat cut out."

"Is that right?"

"Sure is. Want to see my bird?"

"I didn't know you had a pet already."

Max jumped up. Brendan followed him down the hallway. The boy's room included a sewing cabinet and a cutting station along one wall, as if the ex-mother-in-law couldn't bear to let Max have an exclusive space to call his own. It would be just like the old bitch to lord it over Nicole and Max for living here.

Max sat on the single bed. The table next to the bed held a wire cage. Inside the cage, the blue and purple budgerigar stopped pecking at its seed bell to whistle and bob its head. Max poked his finger through the bars. The budgie hopped over and nibbled at Max's fingernail, pausing every now and then to make an irritated, chattering sound.

"Is he angry?" Brendan said.

"I don't know."

"Can he talk?"

"I've said 'hello' to him about a million times but he never says it back."

Brendan approached the cage. The bird let go of Max's fingernail to regard Brendan silently with an arched neck and a single, beady eye. The bird looked ready to flee, but to where? The cage's wire door was closed. There was no other exit.

"His name's Ralph," Max said, "but he's only a baby. We're not sure yet if he's a boy or a girl."

"How will you tell?"

"Um, I guess if he starts spitting eggs out his bum, he's a girl."

Brendan laughed. Max did too. They looked at each other for a time.

Finally, Max said, "Are you really my dad?"

"Yeah."

"How come I never met you before?"

"We've met. You just don't remember me."

"That's what Mum says. She reckons you've been living on the other side of the world."

"Yeah," Brendan said at last. "I was at a place where they don't have phones."

"What about e-mail?"

"They don't have computers there either."

"Geez, you were out in the wild?"

Max looked impressed, thrilled, his eyes big and green. In one way, the boy resembled Nicole; in another, Brendan saw himself. He felt an urge to hug his son, to kiss him, to apologise, over and over, to tell him the truth. He lowered his gaze.

"Listen, mate," he said. "I need to explain something."

Ralph the budgie opened its throat and began to wolf whistle.

Giggling, Max said, "I taught him how to do that."

"Come and get it," shouted Nicole from the kitchen. "Get it while it's hot."

With a jolt, Brendan recognised her words. Back when they were a family, she used to say that exact same phrase every night, even in summer when she was serving up salad. *Get it while it's hot.* Max ran from the room.

"Brendan," Nicole yelled after a time. "Are you coming or not?"

Getting up, he said, "Yeah, I'm on my way."

The dining room table was formally set with placemats, coasters, silver cutlery, napkins; a vase of red and pink roses. The sight choked him up. Nicole and Max were seated already. The last placemat was at the head of the table.

"What are you waiting for?" Max said, grinning. "It's Mum's shepherd's pie."

Brendan sat down. It was the first time they'd all been at a dinner table together since he'd abandoned them. Brendan and Nicole locked eyes. Max grabbed the serving spoon and began to dollop meat and potatoes from the casserole dish onto his plate.

After coffee and cake, Brendan made his goodbyes. Nicole saw him to the door.

At nearly eight p.m., the lone streetlamp failed to illuminate much of the area. When Brendan was almost at his car, someone got out from the driver's side of a vehicle parked a short distance ahead. Brendan grabbed at his jacket pocket, simultaneously remembering that he'd left the Beretta in the glovebox. The person approached. It was Pinch.

Brendan said, "How did you know I was here?"

"When you weren't at your flat, I figured it out."

"Figured it out how? I've never given anyone this address."

"We go back a long way, Danny Boy."

"Huh?"

"When you were a prospect, your mullet put everyone else's to shame."

"What are you talking about?"

"And your beard? Hell's bells, you were quite the sight. I had hair back then too; kept it in a plait most of the time. Remember?"

Distracted, Pinch ran his fingers over the back of his bald, pink scalp and stared off with a faraway gaze. It gave Brendan the creeps.

Grabbing Pinch on the elbow, shaking him as if to wake him up, Brendan said, "What's going on?"

"Itchy is waiting for you at your flat. He's got his bag of tricks with him."

The bag with the pliers and blowtorch. Fear tightened Brendan's guts. He let go of Pinch.

"You lied about Abby," Pinch continued.

"No, I didn't."

"Yeah, you did. You said you tailed him but couldn't get a shot. That's not what happened." Pinch took a step closer. "According to a little birdie, you and Abby had quite the chat in his backyard last night."

Dumbfounded, Brendan said, "How do you know that?"

Pinch gave a sly grin and tapped the side of his nose.

Brendan said, "Are you the one that's been talking to Abby? Telling him about our meetings?"

"If I were you, mate, I'd be more worried about my own skin. The word is you're trying to jump ship."

"Jump ship?" Brendan laughed, frowned. "You mean join the Golden Jackals?"

Pinch nodded.

"No way," Brendan said. "Why would I do that?"

"Because you don't want to be an Overlord any more."

"Yeah, that's right, I want to retire."

"Because you hate Vic's leadership."

"What?" Brendan's head was starting to spin. "No, that's bullshit. I've never spoken a word against the bloke."

"You don't have to. For one thing, look how you carry on in meetings. You put your head down on the table and pretend to fall asleep."

"Huh? I've done that, like, twice maybe."

"You do it all the time. Vic's let it slide because you're a veteran."

"No, shit no. It's not because of Vic. I just hate accounting stuff... numbers and forecasts and crap. I get bored."

"And when was the last time you came to one of our social get-togethers?"

"What? Come on, I'm just tired of whores and drugs. Who gives a shit?"

"We do. You don't come to the get-togethers, you put yourself apart. And the two grand out of your own pocket you were supposed to give to Vic? The unpaid dues from that Bayswater tattoo parlour?"

"What about it? I gave him all the money I took from Farid, didn't I?"

"Not the same thing. Everybody settles debts with Vic straight away. When you didn't pay him straight away with your own money, you undermined his authority. You embarrassed him, Danny Boy. You embarrassed our president in front of the whole club. And now this shit with Abby." Pinch tut-tutted. "Thanks to your heads-up, Abby and Rashid have gone into hiding, the Jackals are on high alert, they've hit some of our places already as payback – God almighty, how the Jackals love molotov cocktails – and to top it off, Vic and Ellery have had to disappear in case of reprisal attacks. The rest of us are too jumpy to go to the Burley in case Jackals bomb the joint. It's fucken turmoil. All of this is seen as your fault. I mean, come on, what are we supposed to think? It looks like you've turned against us."

"I haven't, I swear." Brendan ran his hands through his hair, realised that he was sweating. "Vic thinks I've turned against the club?"

"He sees you as a traitor. Most of us are still on your side – me, of course, and Ellery, a few others – but our votes don't count for much. As president, Vic's got the power of veto."

"So what are you saying?" Brendan said. "That I'm screwed?"

Pinch considered, shrugged, nodded.

"And that's it?" Brendan said.

"Yeah, that's it."

"Shit. What does he want to do?"

"Kill you," Pinch said, then hesitated. "Or let you live, and kill either your kid or your missus."

Brendan's heart almost seized.

15

Steady on, mate, listen," Pinch added, "Ellery's trying to talk him out of the family option. Okay? We all are. Nobody wants sheilas and kids dragged into this. Nobody wants a repeat of the Skulls war. But Vic reckons your punishment has to be severe. He reckons he has to make an example of you in case anyone else in the club is thinking of following your lead, you get me?"

Brendan turned and gazed at his mother-in-law's house. By now, Nicole would be chasing Max into the bathroom; hassling him to get ready for bed.

When he found his voice, he said, "Can you give us a head start?"

"No-one knows I'm here and no-one's going to know. Best of luck, mate."

Pinch offered his hand and Brendan took it. The old man looked upset, tearful, as if he were in mourning already.

Brendan whispered, "Oh fuck, what should I do?"

"I don't know. But whatever it is, Danny Boy, do it fast. If I found this address, it won't take long for other people to find it. You got money?"

"What? Yeah, I guess."

Reaching into a jacket pocket, Pinch took out a sheaf of bills. "You were always a top bloke in my book, Danny Boy," he said. "In a way, I almost feel... I feel kind of responsible. Here."

Pinch handed over the money. Brendan took it.

"Be careful," Pinch said. "Now bugger off while the going's good."

Brendan pocketed the money, slapped Pinch on the arm, then sprinted over his mother-in-law's front lawn and pounded on the door.

"It's me," he yelled over and over, "open up, it's me."

Nicole flung the door wide. "What the hell is wrong with you?" she hissed. "Have you lost your fucking mind?"

Brendan pushed inside and slammed the door. Max, peeking from the lounge room, ducked and ran towards his room.

"You have to get out of here," Brendan said. Clutching Nicole's arm, dragging her down the hallway, he continued, "Pack stuff for you and Max. I'm serious, you can't stay here."

"What did you do?" Nicole wrenched her arm free. "What's going on?"

"I'll tell you in the car."

She must have seen the fear in his eyes. The colour drained from her cheeks.

"It'll be okay," he said, "I promise. But first we've got to leave."

"How much time do we have?"

"I don't know."

"Help Max with his stuff," she said. "I'll be ready in ten minutes."

"Sooner than that."

Nicole hurried to her room. Brendan went into Max's room. The boy was standing against the far wall, his hands clasped together, white-knuckled.

"You got a suitcase?" Brendan said. "A backpack?"

Max didn't answer. Brendan threw open the wardrobe door, found a duffel bag on the top shelf. Lobbing the duffel bag on the bed, he began wrenching clothes off hangers and out of drawers, aiming them at Max.

Brendan said, "Put the clothes in the bag."

"I don't know how to fold anything."

"Forget about that, just shove it in."

With a trembling chin, Max stood motionless, flinching every time a piece of clothing hit against him and fell to the carpet. The budgerigar started chirruping at the top of its lungs. The piercing noise lanced at Brendan's eardrums.

"The clothes," Brendan said. "Put them in the bag now, right now."

Max picked up the articles, one at a time, and began placing them gently, hesitantly, inside the duffel bag.

"Faster," Brendan said. "Would you hurry up? Jesus."

T-shirts, jeans, socks, jocks, shoes, Brendan noted as his heart knocked into his throat, jacket, hat, jumpers, pyjamas. Everything he snatched up, he threw behind him. When he glanced around to check on Max's progress, he found the boy just standing there again, doing nothing, his hands squeezed together.

"What the fuck did I tell you to do?" Brendan shouted.

Max shrank away and let out a long, plaintive wail. Stricken, Brendan went over. The boy actually cringed at his approach. *Christ almighty, I'm such a shithouse father.* Dropping to one knee, he gathered his son against him in a hug. The boy's entire body felt rigid. It occurred to Brendan, fleetingly, that this was the first time he had embraced his child, his only child, in almost four years.

"I'm sorry," Brendan said. "I didn't mean to yell. You're scared, but so am I. People are coming here. They could be here any minute."

He drew back, held Max by his narrow, bony shoulders, and stared at him until Max returned his gaze.

"What people?" Max said at last.

"Bad people. Ones who want to hurt us."

"Hurt us? What for? We haven't done anything."

"Can I tell you later? We've got to leave before the people arrive. Okay?"

Max nodded.

"So can you pack your bag now?" Brendan said.

Sniffing back tears, Max nodded again. When Brendan let go of him, Max snatched at the clothes ranged over the floor and began cramming them hastily into the duffel bag. Brendan ran to the bathroom. There were items inside the cabinet that clearly belonged to Max – a Spiderman toothbrush, a tube of Spongebob Squarepants toothpaste, Junior Chewable Multivitamins – and he swept them up and hurried back to Max's room. Max was shoving the last few items into the duffel bag. Brendan tossed the toiletries on top and pulled the zipper.

"Make tracks," he said, seizing the bag by its straps.

"What about Ralph?"

"Huh?"

"My budgie. He's coming too, isn't he?"

Brendan hesitated.

"I'm not leaving him," Max said, his voice suddenly high, almost hysterical.

"Okay, fine, Ralph comes too."

Max grabbed the cage, which swung madly from the handle. The budgerigar, perhaps stunned by the effects of centrifugal force, stopped its chirruping. As they hastened down the hallway towards the front door, it struck Brendan that he was unarmed. Why hadn't he taken the Beretta from the glovebox before charging in here?

"Nicole," he called. "Whatever you haven't got, leave."

Precious seconds passed. He was about to go to her room when she came out with a suitcase, struggling, banging it against her legs.

"Give it here," Brendan said, slinging the straps of the duffel bag over his shoulder, taking the case from her. "Okay, let's go."

He opened the front door.

And stopped.

It was so quiet and dark out there.

Maybe Pinch had been the lure to draw them from the safety of the house. Maybe Pinch and Itchy were hiding somewhere nearby, guns in hand.

Moving back, pulling the door almost shut again, Brendan scanned the road. The lone streetlamp cast a thin, luminescent outline around his parked Holden, traced the shape of trees planted at intervals along the nature strips, gave the lawn a sickly, grey cast, and left everything else in shadow. If they were lying in wait, he wouldn't be able to see them. His heart gave a lurch.

"Let me go first," he said. "Anything happens, bolt the door and call the cops."

Nicole gripped his arm. "Oh shit, Brendan."

"I'll bring the car down the driveway. Wait for me. Okay?"

"Okay," she whispered.

He stepped out onto the porch. His legs felt stiff, almost locked at the knees. As he jogged across the lawn, he became aware of the blood pressure pulsing in a frantic tempo behind his eyes. He fumbled in his pocket for keys. *Please God, let me get my family to safety, and then I don't care what happens to me.*

Pinch's ute was gone. No other cars were parked in the immediate area. That had to be a good sign. He dumped the suitcase and duffel bag in the Holden's boot. When he got in the driver's side, he took the Beretta from the glovebox and shoved it in his jacket pocket.

This nightmare wouldn't be happening if he'd used the Beretta on Abby.

For a moment, overwhelmed, the realisation nauseated him.

What was the old saying? *No good deed goes unpunished.* But if he had the chance to go back, knowing what he did now, would he kill Abby? Probably not. Did that make him weak? He didn't know.

Cursing, he started the car and kicked the accelerator. Instead of taking the driveway into the carport, he rode over the lawn and parked in front of the porch so that Nicole and Max would have cover. He jumped from the car.

"Come on, let's go," he said.

They didn't move. He grabbed them both and ushered them to the car. Nicole got in the front passenger side. Max climbed into the back with Ralph. As Brendan hopped in behind the wheel, relief surged through him in a great tide, strong enough to make his legs tremble. They'd made it this far, which meant they could get away.

Max said, "Nana's gonna be mad about the grass."

"I'll get her some new grass," Brendan said, buckling his seatbelt. "Don't worry about it."

"She'll be mad anyway."

"Oh, yeah?" Smiling, Brendan turned the wheel hard, gave the accelerator a shove, and churned up mud as he steered back onto the road.

"Shit, what did you do that for?" Nicole said.

"If we're going to make her mad, let's make her ballistic."

He started laughing. Max joined in. When they turned out of the street, Nicole put her hand on Brendan's thigh and began to giggle too, just a little, even though unshed tears stood in her eyes. He could feel her hand shaking.

16

They drove for a long time. Nobody spoke. The radio murmured one song after another. The traffic thinned out. After a while, so did the buildings, houses, signs of the city. They began passing through large tracts of empty land. The occasional farm house, windows lit up against the night, tracked by them in the distance.

"Where are we going?" Nicole said at last.

"Daylesford," Brendan said.

"How come?"

"No club chapters."

He reached into the console for a pack of cigarettes.

Nicole grabbed his wrist. "You can't smoke in the car. What about Max and Ralph?"

Brendan returned the cigarettes to the console. After a while, Nicole took her phone from her handbag and started pressing buttons.

"What are you doing?" he said.

"Texting Mum."

"Don't tell her where we're going."

"Of course I won't. But she'll be back from poker soon and I don't want her to worry." After typing the message, she read out loud, "Max and I are staying overnight with a friend. Sorry about the kitchen mess." She looked at him, as if for approval.

"Fine," he said. "Go ahead and send it."

"Okay, done. That'll keep her happy for a bit." Returning the phone to her bag, she said, "When can Max and I really go home?"

He couldn't think of how to answer.

She said, "What's going on?"

"I don't want Max to hear."

Nicole turned her head towards the back seat. "He's asleep."

Brendan tightened his grip on the steering wheel. A thin fog was rolling across the Western Freeway. At times, the shapes looked almost human, like fleeing ghosts. Then he would run them through with the Holden and rip them apart over the bonnet.

"Please," she said. "You have to tell me."

"Okay, all right. The Golden Jackals are trying to steal territory from us. Vic ordered me to kill their vice-president."

Gasping, her hand flew to her mouth.

"I didn't do it," he hurried to add, "he's alive, I couldn't kill him. But that's the trouble. Vic's after me now. Do you see? I fucked up."

He looked across. Her face seemed ashen. Perhaps that was from the darkness and the reflection of headlights against the grey fog. The car whisked through more apparitions. Brendan felt sick and exhausted.

"If he's after you," she said at last, "then why did Max and I have to run?"

"Because Vic might want things done in a different way."

"Different how?"

Brendan fidgeted in his seat. "Look, when I was a kid, bikies were just mates that liked to ride together. A few of us did the odd job here and there, nothing too big, and we mucked about with drugs for a bit of cash. Shit, I used to courier speed in my fuel tank, remember? Like that ride we did from Sydney, the one where we free-camped? We had a sample; you danced all night in your bra and undies, remember?"

She didn't answer. Brendan cleared his throat.

"Well, it's not like that any more," he continued. "Those days are over. Bikie clubs are criminal gangs now."

"Yeah, I know that already, I read the papers, I watch the news. You still haven't answered my question. What's it got to do with me and Max?"

Brendan wiped sweat from his upper lip. "Vic wants to teach me the kind of lesson that will scare every bloke in the club."

"Oh my God."

"But I'm not going to let anything happen to you or Max. I swear I won't."

"Oh shit, oh God."

"It's all right. I promise it'll be all right."

She began to cry.

"No, listen to me," he said, his voice rising. "Everything's going to be okay."

"Mum?"

Nicole jumped. Brendan did too. They both glanced into the back seat. Max was stretching, rubbing at his eyes, squinting at them.

"Off to sleep again, honey," she said. "Settle yourself down."

"We forgot the seed."

"The what?" Brendan said.

"For Ralph, his birdseed, we forgot to bring it."

"I'll buy him some more," Brendan said. "Don't worry about it. Go to sleep."

"Okay, Dad."

The breath caught in Brendan's throat. *Dad?* He looked around at Nicole. She was shaking her head at him, her trembling lips pressed together. He reached out and took her hand. At first, she tried to pull away. He wouldn't let go. After a while, she closed her fingers around his and squeezed tight.

"Don't be afraid," he whispered. "I'll sort this out."

The illuminated road-sign for the caravan park proclaimed vacancies. They pulled in. At nearly ten p.m., the office was closed. Brendan kept pressing the bell while the Holden idled in the driveway and Nicole watched him from the passenger side window. At last, an exasperated middle-aged woman came to the door.

"We need a cabin," Brendan said, "two-bedroom with an inside dunny if there's any spare."

Since it was winter, off-season, they had plenty of cabins to choose from. Brendan opted for one by the lake. Shaped like a brick with a flat tin roof, the wooden cabin had an open-plan lounge with kitchenette, two bedrooms, bathroom, and a separate toilet. Nicole cranked up the heater, put the kettle on and fussed with sachets of tea and coffee while Brendan carried in the luggage, the budgie, and finally Max.

Brendan took him into the second bedroom. There were two sets of bunks. As he placed the boy on one of the bottom bunks, he mumbled something in his sleep that Brendan didn't catch.

"Shh," he whispered. "Go back to your dreams."

He removed Max's shoes and pulled up the blankets. In the half-light, his son's eyelids were delicately veined, almost translucent, as fragile as butterfly wings. Brendan gazed at him for a long time. Then he left the room and gently shut the door.

In the lounge room, Nicole had the duffel bag on the couch and was hunting through it, tossing items of clothing to the cushions on either side. Brendan dropped into the nearby armchair and lit a smoke.

"Your coffee's on the kitchen bench," she said. "I can't find Bluey. Did you forget to bring him?"

"Who's Bluey?"

"Max's bunny. It would've been on his pillow."

"A bunny was on his pillow?"

"Yeah; you know, a stuffed toy rabbit."

"What's he got a toy rabbit for?"

"To take with him to bed."

Brendan stopped his exhalation of cigarette smoke mid-stream. "Are you shitting me?"

"It settles him down."

"He sleeps with a toy?"

"Yeah, so?" Straightening up, she turned to face him. "There's nothing wrong with that, it helps him unwind."

"He's eight years old."

She crossed her arms, stony-faced. "Six."

"Okay, six. Why do you still let him have a toy, for Christ's sake?"

"You know what?" she said, her voice shrill. "I don't have to explain myself to you. It's none of your business."

Brendan stood up. "Hey, I'm his father."

"Oh, yeah? For how long this time?"

That took the wind out of him. She hurried towards the master bedroom.

"Nicole," he began. "Wait."

She closed the door. Falling back into the armchair, Brendan dragged hard on the cigarette and rubbed at his temples with his free hand, trying to stave off the headache that was tightening like a band. Why could he never say the right thing at the right time? Or at least keep his mouth shut? They'd had arguments like this a thousand times, a million times. Didn't he know any better by now?

Fatigue overtook him. The desire to jump in the car and run almost got the better of him. Instead, he stamped out the cigarette on the lino – *fuck it* – and lit another. By the time he smoked that one down to the filter, he felt calmer, more like himself again.

He stood up and went to the master bedroom. The closed door

looked like a tough adversary. Softly, he tapped his knuckles on it. No answer. He'd suggest that she come back to the lounge room because their drinks were getting cold. As he turned the handle, he braced himself. She was probably getting ready to throw something at him: a lamp, a clock radio, her shoe. He cracked the door, waited, and then pushed it open the whole way.

She was crying, which he didn't expect, sprawled full-length on the bed, hugging a pillow, sobbing hard enough to break his heart.

"No, come on, I'm sorry, okay?" He sat down on the mattress and started rubbing at her shoulders. "I didn't mean it. I didn't mean any of it. You're a great mum. If Max sleeps with a toy, that's fine by me, okay? You hear me? Nicole?"

She stopped crying, lifted her head, sniffed, and ran her nose along her arm. Then, slowly and with great effort, she rolled onto her back. Her staring eyes looked at him, vacant. *If only she were chucking things.* Fear raised the hair on his neck. Lying so still with her face blank and masklike, she seemed already dead.

"Nicole," he whispered. "I'm so sorry."

She held out her arms. He lay down next to her and they embraced. Her hair smelt like cherries, which meant she was still using the same shampoo he remembered. If he relaxed, emptied his mind, he could pretend that no time had passed at all. For a few minutes, it was like they were back in their queen-sized bed at home, with Max down the hallway, first bedroom on the left, asleep in his cot.

She pulled away, breaking his reverie.

"How long are we staying here?" she said.

"Just a few days," he said, although he didn't really know.

"What'll I tell work?"

"That you're sick."

"I'll have to ring the school too."

"Some time off won't hurt him."

She sat up. "Aw shit, what am I going to tell Mum?"

"Whatever you want."

"The truth?"

He bit at the inside of his lip. "Maybe not that."

17

Later, he dreamed of the accident. The Holden flipped and hit the dam. Countless bubbles rushed at him, streaking with great speed and purpose.

Follow the bubbles.

Were his eyes open?

Yes. The realisation surprised him. Yes, his eyes were open.

Somehow, he was out of the car. The bubbles were streaming away in a straight line, swirling up, up, up, while he drifted down, down, down. He knew he should start swimming but the water felt so warm. He continued to sink. At the very limit of his vision, he saw bubbles starting to break across a surface that was far away from him, as far away as a night sky full of stars, and then he realised that he was not just free of the car but free of the dam too, and now the planet. He was a wisp of fog moving unfettered through the universe.

"Can I get in with you?"

Startled, Brendan woke up.

In the grey half-light, Max was standing by the bed. On the other side of the mattress, Nicole stirred, gave a little snore, turned over. It took Brendan a moment to remember where he was. According to the clock, it was just on quarter to two in the morning. He and Nicole had gone to bed sometime around midnight. She had cleaned her teeth first, and handed over the brush. You know it's true love when you can share a toothbrush without freaking out.

113

"Dad?" Max said.

"What is it, mate?"

"Can I sleep with you?"

"Huh? Yeah, sure." Brendan made some room, flipped back the blankets, and saw that Max was wearing pyjamas. "You got changed?" Brendan said. "How long have you been awake?"

"A while," Max said, climbing in. "Is this your house?"

"Nah, mate, it's a cabin in a caravan park."

"Oh. Where's Ralph?"

"In the kitchen. Mum put a tea-towel over the cage for him, so he's all right."

Nicole's breathing had changed. Brendan knew that she was awake and listening. He arranged the blankets over his son, tucking them tightly.

"I'm sorry I forgot your rabbit," he continued.

Max sighed. "I don't always sleep with him, you know. Like when I stay with friends or go on camp, I leave him at home. I can sleep without him if I want to."

"It's okay."

"Nana says I'm too big for Bluey."

"Yeah, well, Nana's pretty old. She doesn't know what she's talking about half the time."

Max giggled.

"You think you could nod off?" Brendan added. "We don't want to disturb your mum."

Max wriggled about, shifted his head on the pillow, and lay still. His breathing became quiet and regular. After a time, Brendan felt Nicole slide across the mattress. She lay close behind him, put an arm around his waist, and kissed his bare back. Soon, her gentle snoring started up again.

Brendan stayed awake and listened to the both of them sleeping.

In the morning, upon opening the lounge room curtains, Max discovered there was a playground directly across from their cabin. He wanted to play on the slides and swings immediately but Nicole insisted that they eat first.

There was no food in the cabin. They went out for breakfast at a cafe that overlooked Lake Daylesford. Max, fixated on the ducks, didn't notice that Nicole was quiet and withdrawn. Brendan tried to hold her hand across the table but she wouldn't allow it. After eggs and pancakes, they drove around town, and ended up spending an hour or so at an outdoor mini-golf course once Max decided he was getting bored.

The course was eighteen holes, all of them too hard for Max, who had never played mini-golf before. They formed two teams: Brendan and Max versus Nicole. Each hole was themed around something Australian – the Sydney Harbour Bridge, saltwater crocodiles, Ned Kelly, the Outback – which gave Brendan plenty of topics to talk about with Max, since Nicole was hardly speaking.

"You okay?" Brendan said.

Nicole cut her eyes at him and looked away.

Grey clouds hung low overhead. The rain held off but the wind was icy. By the time they finished the course – the boys winning by four strokes – Max's cheeks were bright red and chapped.

In the car, Brendan said, "Where to now?"

"An ice cream parlour," Max said.

"No, the cabin," Nicole said. "We have stuff to figure out, remember?"

"Look, I got to get some clothes first, so I'll drop you back, I won't be long."

"Can you buy me rocky road in a cone?"

"Aw, come off it, mate," Brendan said, trying to laugh, nudging at Nicole, "it's too bloody freezing for ice cream, isn't it?"

Nicole averted her face and stared out the window, her arms folded tight against her body. For the few minutes it took to drive to the caravan park, Max kept up a happy chatter about the mini-golf, but Brendan was only half-listening. Nicole's moods were changing too fast for him to keep track. What was she feeling right now? He had no idea.

After driving them back to the cabin, Brendan headed off alone to the town centre. He came back an hour later with a shopping bag containing a shirt, a packet of underpants, three pairs of socks, and some toiletries. In his other hand, he carried a tub of ice cream. Nicole was sitting in the armchair, reading something off her mobile phone, absorbed and focused.

"I couldn't find an ice cream place," Brendan said, as he put the tub on the kitchen bench. "So I stopped off at a supermarket and got this for him. Where is he?"

She pointed. He looked out the lounge room window and saw Max in the nearby playground, rocking back and forth on one of the swings. When Brendan turned around again, Nicole was standing right there with her phone held up to his face as if she were getting ready to hit him with it.

"The fuck?" he said, recoiling. "What are you, a ninja?"

"Read it."

"Huh?" He took the phone from her.

"The news article, read it."

He sat on the couch and stared at the screen. The headline read, *Bikie War: double shootings.* Brendan's stomach turned over. He closed his eyes.

"Read it," Nicole demanded.

Taking a deep breath, he obeyed.

The violent feud involving two of Melbourne's largest bikie gangs reignited overnight when an alleged member of the Overlords was shot dead in his car at approximately eleven p.m. in the eastern suburb of Scoresby. At about midnight, an alleged member of the Golden Jackals suffered gunshot wounds during a home invasion in Mulgrave. The man is currently in Dandenong Hospital under police guard in a critical condition.

After the two shootings, a flurry of crimes occurred across the eastern suburbs throughout the night, including a car bombing and various arson attacks. While investigations are still ongoing, police sources are confident that these crimes are linked to the ongoing power struggle between the long-established Overlords and the up-and-coming Golden Jackals.

"Does it say who's dead and who's alive?" Brendan said.

"Just keep reading."

"Can't you tell me instead?"

She glared at him. Brendan sighed, bent his head to the screen.

The ABC has been told that the initial shooting was retaliation for a botched attempt by the Overlords on Sunday night to assassinate the vice-president of the Golden Jackals, Abdullah 'Abby' Hanoush. The would-be assassin is thought to be veteran Overlord member Brendan 'Danny Boy' Reilly, who is missing, presumed dead.

Brendan jolted, sat up straight. "Hey," he said, "they used my name. Isn't that libel or whatever? Some defamatory shit, what's it called? Slander? Aw Christ... your mum's going to flip when she sees this."

"Forget about that," Nicole said. "We're safe. Everyone thinks you're dead."

"No. This journo thinks I'm dead."

"Can't we run?"

"To where? Clubs have chapters all over Australia. I've been an Overlord for nearly thirty years. There's probably not a bikie alive that doesn't know my name, and every one of them would turn me in to the Overlords for a bounty."

"Then what? What are we going to do?"

Brendan scrolled through the article. "Shit, how long is this?"

"It goes on for pages."

"Who was the Overlord that got killed? Was it Vic?"

"They didn't say. But they mention Vic… they reckon he's a warmonger, that the clubs in Melbourne were more or less peaceful until he came along."

"Yeah, well, they got that right." Brendan put the phone on the arm of the couch. "This'll be our second war in eight years because of him."

"Is Ellery Christensen still vice-president?"

"Yeah."

"He's a reasonable guy. What's he think about the whole thing?"

Brendan shrugged. "He doesn't like it, but tough titties. Vic's the boss."

Nicole came over and sat next to him on the couch. Something about the expression on her face made him tense up.

"We could get out of this," she said, "if Ellery was president."

"Maybe so, but it'll never happen. Vic wouldn't step down."

She nodded. "And that's why you have to kill him."

18

Brendan stared at her, gave a half-hearted laugh. "You want me to kill Stevan Petrovic?" he said. "That's crazy talk."

"No, it isn't. If Ellery was in charge, he'd call off the hits on us, wouldn't he?"

"I suppose, yeah."

"And he'd probably let you retire too, wouldn't he?"

"He seemed open to the idea."

"And if Ellery was president, there wouldn't be any war. He'd broker a deal with the Golden Jackals, right?" She took hold of his hand. "Everybody wins."

"Except us," he said. "If I kill my own president, every patched Overlord, associate and prospect would want to skin me alive, and come after you and Max for the cherry on top."

"Yeah, but only if they thought it was you that killed him."

"Huh? So it's not me that kills him?"

Nicole let go of his hand and grabbed his chin for a moment, forcing him to meet her gaze. Her eyes were hectic, animated, standing out against bloodless cheeks.

"Yes, it's you that kills him," she said, "but you make it look like the Golden Jackals did it. You see? Both gangs are fighting tit-for-tat right now. Who's to say the Jackals don't get lucky and tag Vic?"

He thought about that while biting on a knuckle. Nicole waited.

"No," he said, shaking his head. "The Jackals would still be after me."

"What for? Abby Hanoush is alive. The Jackals don't have any beef with you."

"Shit, you don't know these blokes."

"Isn't it worth a try? For my sake? For Max?"

"I just don't think it would work, that's all." Brendan lit a smoke. "Even with Vic dead, there are Overlords that'd shoot me on his account."

"But everyone will have to obey Ellery once he's president."

"You're forgetting loyalty. Some of the blokes would chop off their right arm for Vic. Blokes like Itchy, you know him, the big Maori bastard with red hair?"

"Okay, so what the hell do we do?"

He didn't – couldn't – say anything.

She shoved at him. "Tell me," she said. "How are you going to protect us? What's your plan?"

"I don't have one."

She crumpled a little, dropped her forehead to one palm. Brendan got up, paced around, and stood by the window. Max was climbing up the chute of the slide, grabbing the sides, making slow progress as if scaling a cliff face. Every now and then, his sneakers would slip. He tumbled to the bottom more than once. Eventually, Brendan crushed the cigarette against the window sill and sat next to Nicole on the couch. This whole time, perhaps two or three minutes, she hadn't spoken a word.

"I can't do it," he said at last. "I can't kill Vic."

"Yes, you can."

"No, I'm not a killer," Brendan said. "I couldn't kill Abby, remember?"

"You killed Waldo."

Brendan froze.

"Waldo," she continued, "the sergeant-at-arms from the Skulls. You got him in his driveway while he was closing the garage, didn't you?"

Brendan couldn't look at her. If he tried to deny it, she would see the lie in his face. His heart galloped. Stalling, he lit another cigarette.

"We've known each other twenty years," she said, resting a hand on his leg. "I understand the life a hell of a lot better than you think."

"How long have you known?"

"Since the day after it happened. I saw the news reports and put two and two together. You had blood on your clothes. I knew it wasn't from a nosebleed. And those nightmares… the things you'd say in your sleep."

Brendan stamped the cigarette into the floor. "Why didn't you bring it up?"

"I was for waiting for you to tell me."

"If you knew I'd killed someone, why didn't you leave?"

"I don't know," she said. "I guess I loved you too much."

"Do you still love me?"

She grabbed his hand and squeezed it.

The front door clattered open, startling them both. Max, grinning, his cheeks flushed, ran straight to Brendan and began tugging on his wrist.

"Dad, there's a cool seesaw, come on, let's go."

"Sweetie, wait," Nicole said, "your father and I are talking."

Brendan stood up. "Take Mum instead. I've got to go out for a minute."

"Where are you going?" Nicole said, with a fresh and sudden fear in her eyes.

"It's okay, I'll be back soon."

Brendan drove into town, bought a pre-paid mobile phone, and called Ellery. The number rang and rang, then went to message bank.

"It's Danny Boy," Brendan said after the beep. "I know you're screening calls. I'll ring back in a minute."

Sitting in his parked car, Brendan hung up and checked his watch. Nearly midday. Vehicles coasted along the main street, some moving in and out of the central parking bays. Across the road on the footpath, a scruffy-looking busker strummed an acoustic guitar while a few people stood around. The occasional passerby threw coins.

Brendan looked at his watch again, rang the number. Ellery picked up.

"Danny Boy?" Ellery said.

"Yeah, it's me."

"I'm not getting a caller ID."

"This is a pre-paid."

"I see," Ellery said. "How are you doing in these troubled times?"

"All right, I guess. How're things with you?"

"Not good, as you're probably aware. They got Kingfisher with a shotgun."

An older man with a full beard and shaved head, Kingfisher, as road captain, had been responsible for club tours and the maintenance of club vehicles. When the Overlords travelled en masse, he was always at Vic's side. While road captain was an important position, it was a non-executive one, making the hit a strange choice.

Brendan said, "Why in hell would the Jackals pop Kingfisher?"

"You tell me."

"Huh? How would I know?"

"Danny Boy, for old times' sake, please explain why Kingfisher was a target."

Brendan tightened his grip on the phone. "I'm not in bed with the Jackals."

"Rumour says otherwise."

"Ellery, I swear."

"Danny Boy, you were face to face with Abby on Sunday night. When I saw you Monday, you told me you didn't shoot him because you couldn't get near him."

"Look, I'm sorry for lying, okay? I didn't know how to tell you I'd fucked up. And Jesus, with Itchy there too? Maybe with his blowtorch on hand?"

Ellery paused. "I want to believe you."

"I'm telling you the truth."

"In any case, it's not up to me."

"Can't you straighten things out with Vic? Put in a good word?"

Ellery made a sound like a laugh. "Bottom line, Sunday night, you talked to Abby, perhaps not for the first time. The Jackals know a lot about our business."

"Yeah, I talked to Abby. We were face to face, like you say, but I had the gun in my hand, ready to finish him. Then his kids started singing."

"They what?"

"Shit, Ellery. His kids, okay? I just couldn't do it."

"Because you're a family man yourself?"

"Right."

"I understand. How are Nicole and Max?"

Brendan didn't answer.

"Relax," Ellery said. "Vic says plenty of things he doesn't mean. Come out of hiding and we'll talk about it."

Brendan hung up.

He thought about Nicole and Max. Then he lit a cigarette and thought about them some more. Smoke after smoke, as the lunchtime crowds swelled and thinned, he thought about them.

When Brendan returned to the caravan park, he stopped at reception. Behind the counter was a middle-aged man with a creased, pouchy face and wavy black hair shot through with grey.

Looking up from his newspaper, the man said, "Checking in?"

"Nah, we're already in a cabin. We got here last night."

"Everything to your liking?"

"Yeah, great," Brendan said. "Listen… is there a used-car yard around here?"

"As a matter of fact, my wife wants to sell her Toyota Corolla."

"Oh yeah?"

"She's kept it in good nick. To be honest, though, it's twenty-three years old."

"I don't care as long as it goes."

"It goes like a thousand fleeting gazelles." The man stood up, taking off his glasses. "Automatic, four cylinder, one-point-six litre, two months' rego. Interested? The mileage is very low, considering its age."

Brendan patted at his jacket, feeling the wad of Pinch's money wedged in the inside pocket. He said, "How much?"

The man paused, as if considering. "Sixteen hundred."

"Thirteen, cash."

"Done."

"When can I have a look at it?"

"How about now? It's here in the park."

Smiling, the man unlocked the little swing door in the countertop. Brendan followed him outside.

19

Before he had time to reach for the cabin door, Nicole had already opened it. She must have been watching for him through the windows.

"Where have you been?" she said.

"Let me inside, I need a coffee."

She opened the door wide and went to the kitchen bench, flipping the switch on the kettle. Max was sitting cross-legged on the floor a short distance from the television, watching a cartoon. The volume was up high.

"Mate," Brendan called out, "you'll hurt your eyes that close to the telly."

"That's a myth," Max shouted back.

"Hey, what did I just tell you? Don't argue with me."

Huffing, rolling his eyes, Max scooched back a few centimetres, then folded his hands in his lap again and returned his attention to the screen.

Brendan leaned an elbow on the bench. "Can you believe this kid?"

"No, he's right," Nicole said. "That theory is horseshit."

"What? Since when?"

She pursed her lips. While she made instant coffee, Brendan turned to the cage at the far end of the bench and watched the budgerigar. It was biting at a small hanging mirror, jingling the attached silver bell.

"Max," Brendan called. "Forget the telly and let your bird out to play."

"Leave it," Nicole hissed. "Can't he watch TV any more?"

"Budgies don't know what windows are," Max called back. "Ralph'll try to fly through one of them and break his neck."

Brendan didn't know what to say. Max shrugged one shoulder and went back to the cartoon. Nicole slid the coffee mug along the bench. Brendan picked it up.

"Thanks," he said, and took a sip. It tasted stale, flavourless.

"Are you going to tell me what's going on or not?"

He put down the mug and pushed it away. Out of his pocket, he grabbed the Holden's key and registration papers and held them out. Finally, she accepted them.

"I'm giving you the Commodore," he said.

"What for?"

"I've bought a Corolla."

She regarded him sideways. "Aren't we driving back to Melbourne together?"

"I'll go first, tomorrow morning. You and Max stay here. Once you know it's safe, leave in the Commodore."

"How will I know it's safe? Will you call me?"

Brendan took out his key ring, twisted off another key. "This opens my storage locker. I'll give you the address in a minute; I've got the card in my wallet. Keep whatever you want, sell whatever you want. Everything is yours. You'll be able to get about ten grand for the Triumph Tiger, all right? Don't accept anything less than ten."

"I don't understand. Where will you be?"

"Open every bag before you toss it," he said, offering her the key. "Number one, there's a brown airline bag with about twelve grand inside. For fuck's sake, don't hand that over to an op shop."

"You're scaring me."

"No, it's okay."

"So you're planning to do what we talked about? You'll take care of Vic?"

But he was on a roll now and couldn't stop. Out of his jacket, he took the remainder of Pinch's money and peeled off a couple of one-hundred dollar bills, stuffing them in his jeans pocket.

"Here's about three and a half," he said, dropping the remaining notes on the kitchen bench. "This is all yours too."

She stepped back from him, her eyes wide. "Baby, I'm scared."

"Don't worry. I'd never let anything happen to you and Max. You know I love you, right?"

She turned her face. Brendan reached across the bench and held her hand.

He said, "From the moment I saw you at that pub, you and your big hair, I fell for you. Remember how Brodie shoved that franger at us?"

"Yeah, the dirty bastard."

"You still got that denim jacket?"

"The one with the shoulder pads?" She gave a wobbly half-smile. "No way."

He pulled her close. Dropping his face to her neck, he whispered, "I'm sorry for the shitty things I've done."

"I know."

"If I could do it over, I would."

"You did all right," she said, and kissed him. Her cheeks had tears on them.

That night, in bed, they made love. Afterwards, lying in his arms, she said, "What made you get sober and come back to us?"

"I don't know."

"Bullshit."

"Look, I can't explain it."

"Just tell me."

"All right," he said. "I pranged my car into a dam and almost drowned."

"Like a near-death experience?" she said, propping herself on one elbow. "Wow, I've read about them; they're intense. Did you see God, like a big white light?"

"No. I saw you and Max."

Her breath caught. He brushed a tendril of hair behind her ear, traced her jaw with a fingertip.

20

On Wednesdays, the Burleywood Creek Hotel didn't open until eleven a.m. At just after nine, the only cars in the parking area out front belonged to the kitchen staff, likely getting ready for the day's lunchtime crowd. There were no club member vehicles. Like Pinch had said, the Overlords were avoiding the Burley – and probably other haunts – for fear of ambushes from the Jackals.

Driving slowly across the gravel, Brendan coasted the Toyota Corolla through the car park. He kept his gaze on the thick stands of gum trees that surrounded the property, his free hand on the Beretta 9mm, the slide already racked and a bullet in the chamber. On the left-hand side of the Burley, marked with a Staff Only sign, lay a narrow track. Brendan took it.

Once behind the hotel, the track widened into a gravelled area for the storage outbuildings. Brendan drove to the furthest corner and parked behind the old incinerator.

The day was cold; about eight degrees according to the radio. Brendan decided to cut the engine – and the heater – so that he could hear the approach of car tyres or people on foot. He wound down the driver's window. The only sounds were the peeping of bellbirds high overhead, the rustle of wet leaves in the breeze. The air carried the faint aroma of wood smoke.

The pre-paid mobile lay on the passenger seat. He picked it up and put it down again. Next, he lit a cigarette.

Early that morning, he'd left the caravan park while Nicole and Max had still been sleeping. They must be awake by now. What would they be doing? Perhaps they were having breakfast at a cafe. Or Nicole was frying up eggs and bacon; they had discovered last night that the caravan park sold a few basic groceries.

Brendan flipped the cigarette butt out the Toyota's window, grabbed the mobile, and dialled. The phone rang twice.

"Yeah," Vic said.

Brendan clamped his jaw. "I thought you'd be screening your calls like Ellery."

"Danny Boy? Fuck, where are you?"

A distant door slammed. Brendan looked around. Out of the rear of the Burley came a woman in a full-length white apron. Without seeming to notice the Toyota Corolla, she entered the pantry building. Moments later, she exited with a big red can in both hands and went back inside the pub.

"Danny Boy, are you there?"

"Yeah," Brendan said, "I'm waiting at the Burley."

"Hah, you expect me to believe that?"

"I'm near the incinerator, parked in a gold Toyota."

"With what? A bomb? You must think I'm stupid."

Brendan hung up, dropped the phone to the passenger seat, and lit another cigarette. Some people were lucky, he knew that. Others worked hard and never got a break, he knew that too. Bad luck happened more often than not. Life wasn't fair. But Nicole had loved him, as it turned out, even though he hadn't deserved it. Then there was Max. When Max was older and a father himself, he might appreciate that a man without options sometimes has to choose the lesser of two evils.

Smoke after smoke, Brendan watched the mirrors.

Finally, he heard the distinctive notes of the Clubsport engine. It made him think about his own car lost in the dam. He'd died that night, he realised now, had lost his life down there in the murk. The few weeks ever since had been a period of grace. He wondered if Nicole would ever understand that. In the Toyota's mirrors, Itchy advanced through the trees holding a shotgun. Other men crept in the shadows.

"Danny Boy," Itchy called. "Throw any weapons out of the car."

For a second, Max's birth came to mind. After a long and terrible labour, the baby had slithered out in a rush of blood and fluid. Max had cried his first breath as dark water pooled across the floor of the hospital room. Life had felt so close to death.

Is he okay? Nicole had murmured, exhausted.

Yeah, he's beautiful, Brendan had replied as the nurse put Max into his arms.

"Danny Boy," Itchy yelled.

Brendan had never believed in God or heaven. None of it mattered now. Up and out through the universe. He closed his eyes.

Follow the bubbles.

Brendan put the gun to his head and pulled the trigger.

131

RONNIE AND RITA

A NOVELLA
BY
DEBORAH SHELDON

Cohesion Press

2013

1

Let me try to explain.

My name is Ronald Brian Spooner, fifty-three years old, single, no living relatives. I mow lawns at a retirement village in Melbourne's outer east that's about five kilometres down the road from my house. The village has two hundred units arranged on a giant estate featuring parks, landscaped gardens, dedicated picnic areas, the works. They have a permanent grounds-keeping staff of six men, not counting the subcontractors like me. This village is where I met Rita McNaughton.

It was the first Wednesday of September, the start of spring. I'd just cut back Mrs Caldecott's azalea when the old dear tottered out and asked if I would mind re-hanging the doors on a couple of her kitchen cupboards. She said she'd pay me five dollars, but I have a soft spot for her and offered no charge. I carry a toolbox in my ute for little jobs like that, and grabbed a set of screwdrivers. On the porch, I made moves to take off my boots. Mrs Caldecott told me not to worry because the cleaning lady hadn't done the floors yet, so we went inside. Mrs Caldecott retired to her bedroom and shut the door.

I turned towards the kitchen. There was the cleaning lady, sponging the benches with a cloth, a bucket of cleaning products on the floor nearby. Her tracksuit pants had holes in the knees, and the ripped neck of her t-shirt was wide enough to show every freckle on her chest. She was about thirty years old, I guessed, and short, with the lean, hard body of the outdoors type, as if she belonged on a farm throwing hay bales off a tractor.

She stopped and glared at me. "Are you going to mess up my fucken floor?"

Her eyes were stone chips. I shucked my boots and held onto them for a while, until her sneer made me redden and look for an escape. Finally, I put my boots upon a newspaper folded on the kitchen table, hoping that Mrs Caldecott wouldn't notice or, if she did, wouldn't mind, then I edged towards the cupboards, dropping my gaze safely to the floor. But the cleaning lady was barefoot, her feet as dainty as a baby's, a ring glittering on one of her little toes, and I had to look away again. This time it happened to be at the fridge, which had a magnetised real estate calendar holding up a bunch of shopping coupons. I pretended that the coupons were interesting. Out of the corner of my eye, I could see her smirking, studying my face.

She said, "You the biddy's son, or what?"

"I'm one of the caretakers."

"And what's your name, Mr Caretaker?"

"Ronald Spooner. I'm very pleased to meet you, ma'am."

She screwed up her nose. "Ma'am? Aw, come off it, mate. Just call me Rita. Rita McNaughton."

The cupboard doors under the sink hung like crooked teeth. The floor was wet from mopping, and soaked my socks. I mumbled for Rita to move to one side and she took a step, but that was all, and started up with her bench-wiping again. I squatted and opened one of the cupboard doors. My elbow brushed against her every time I worked the screwdriver, and the buzzing of blood got louder in my ears.

"You here every Wednesday?" she said. "I usually clean on Mondays, but I was sick this week. What do they pay you?"

I told her.

She scoffed, and said, "Guess it's my shout for lunch today."

When I didn't answer, she continued, "They do a three-course meal up at the dining room for spare change. Don't you know?"

Of course I knew. I've been mowing lawns at that retirement village for thirty-seven years. But she wasn't serious about the lunch invitation, I thought, she couldn't possibly mean it as anything but a joke, so I didn't answer.

One of the screws on the last cupboard hinge had a stripped thread, and would take some doing to ease out. I tried to focus. My elbow repeatedly grazed Rita as she kept edging towards me, until at last, my heart blatting in my ears, she pressed her thigh hard against my shoulder. All the heady notes of her body wafted over me – cinnamon, salty loam, fresh bread, the sea – and I had to drop the screwdriver, grab my boots, and yell goodbye to Mrs Caldecott as I slammed through the fly-wire door to freedom.

Rita's voice rang out as I stepped off the porch: "See you there at noon."

The words pinned me like a spear through the chest.

See you there at noon.

For the rest of the morning, I mowed, pruned, clipped, trimmed, bagged, hauled, sweated, grunted, and played Rita's words and gestures over and over in my head, agonising about what to do. If I met her for lunch, we would be eating together. That qualified as a date. She would have certain expectations.

At eleven-thirty, I went into the dining hall, a box with a flat tin roof and double doors. The entrance foyer has brochures and notices pinned along yard-long corkboards listing tai chi and swimming classes, day trips to the Yarra Valley, slide nights, cookery lessons, book clubs; a hundred ways to pass the time until life gives up and lets you go. Through another pair of doors is the dining hall proper with its rows of orange plastic tables and chairs, and at the far wall, the toilets. I headed straight to the men's room.

I washed my arms and face, shampooed my hair with liquid soap and sat under the hot blast of the electric hand-dryer, beat out the dirt on my uniform and scraped at flecks of mown grass with my fingernails, mopped at stains with wet paper towels, washed my hands again. After cleaning up as best as I could, there was still about four minutes to go. I locked myself in one of the cubicles and tried to calm down.

At noon, most of the tables were taken.

Rita wasn't there.

I leaned against a wall and faked looking busy with my mobile phone. At ten past, I realised in a sickening rush that she'd been making fun of me after all, but deadpan, so that I wouldn't twig until now.

I was on my way out just as Rita barged through the entrance foyer, her smile hooking the breath in my throat.

"Let's eat, I'm starving," she said, slapping me on the arm.

Without waiting, she crossed to the servery window and started chatting with Bev, the head cook. I trailed behind. Rita ordered for me and I suppose she paid too: pumpkin soup, quiche and salad, sticky date pudding.

We sat at a table and she talked and I listened, but I couldn't tell you one word of our conversation. I was too busy watching her and those fern-green eyes, and the way her auburn hair cow-licked straight up from her forehead and fell down again in frizzled curls to her shoulders. Her teeth were pointy and off-white, and she licked her lips constantly when she spoke as if those loud, strapping words booming from her mouth dried her out.

When she left, she touched me on the hand and said, "See you later."

The week dragged until the following Wednesday. Rita usually cleaned on Mondays so I knew I'd never see her again. Nevertheless, I made sure my uniform was washed Tuesday night, and I packed a spare so I could change before lunch, just in case. I put a can of deodorant in my bag, too. Later in bed, turning from one side to the other until dawn, I rehearsed the kind of conversation I could have with her, memorising a few opening lines, practising my smile into the dark.

Wednesday morning, I dawdled at Mrs Caldecott's for as long as I could. Rita didn't show. I was eating lunch in the ute, trying my best to swallow bites of peanut butter sandwich, pondering what to do about the sad, hollow ache in my guts, when Rita tapped on the driver's side window.

"It's your shout today, Ronnie," she said, grinning.

We went to the dining hall, walking the path side by side without touching; even so, I could somehow feel her, a radiating, penetrating presence like the hot bite of sunshine against naked skin. Over roast pork and apple sauce, she told me she'd swapped her cleaning day to Wednesdays. It was, I think, the most wondrous thing that anyone had ever said to me.

And that's how the whole nightmare started.

The beginning of the end for me, for her.

For everybody.

2

We had lunch at the dining hall one more Wednesday before Rita asked me to her place. She wrote out the address on a paper serviette. I knew the street. It was about half a kilometre from the retirement village off the main road, the kind of street you see everywhere in the outer Melbourne suburbs, full of single-storey brick bungalows with the carport set back on the block to showcase the dying patch of weeds that serves as a lawn.

At eight o'clock sharp that night, I pulled into Rita's street and parked outside her address. I was to take the garden path to the left, since the one to the right led to the landlords' front door, which Rita had warned me to avoid at all costs. Walking along her path started my nerves jangling again. At her porch, a square half-metre of terracotta tiles in front of a bland yellow door, I stood there, preparing myself to ring the bell, mentally drilling my topics of discussion, my throwaway asides, when the door suddenly opened.

"Come in, Ronnie," she said, and headed back to the couch.

The one-bedroom units at the retirement village were small, certainly, but Rita's place was absolutely tiny. I could see the whole thing from where I stood without turning my head: living room and kitchenette, bedroom through one open door, bathroom through the other. That was it. The remaining door off the living room, locked and bolted, presumably led to the rest of the house where her landlords resided.

I stepped in. Rita, barefoot again, wearing a singlet and skimpy pair of bib-and-brace shorts, was already on the couch. I had nowhere to sit but next to her. The couch didn't have springs and the foam rubber collapsed under my weight, tipping Rita towards me. The four walls crowded so close I could have touched them. I stared at the portable television on the bench and wished she'd turn it on. Everything I'd planned to say had gone straight out of my head, so I sat there, gormless, and began to sweat through my shirt.

"Did you find the place okay?" she said.

Her voice was hushed. I supposed she didn't want the landlords to hear so I kept my voice down too.

"Yes," I said. "One of my customers lives on the corner."

From the coffee table, she picked up two glasses brimming with red wine and held one out. I don't drink red but I took it anyway. She looked me over until my face burned. For something to do, I took a gulp from the glass, the wine sour and woody.

"I've never seen you without your navy uniform," she said. "You scrub up all right, don't you?"

Then she sipped at her wine and arranged one leg so she could fiddle with her toes. On the littlest toe was that ring again, glittering in the fading rays from the window, picking up and amplifying the meagre lamp light. She kept turning it, around and around. I wanted to put the point of my tongue against it and taste the metal, tart as a copper penny, warmed by her body heat.

And then I noticed the silence stretching on.

Alarmed, I looked around for a talking point. There were no pictures on the walls, no framed photographs, no personal knick-knacks of any kind, as if Rita McNaughton had dropped out of the sky, completely and utterly alone. As utterly alone as me.

"Quite a dump, isn't it?" she said, startling me. "There's fuck-all money in cleaning houses, like you didn't already know."

"Oh? Well, I'm sorry. Have you thought about doing something else?"

"Like what? I've done most of the other shit jobs already." She pulled a face, and continued, while counting on her fingers, "I've mucked out cow sheds, shovelled bolts on the nightshift, hosed out a butcher's shop, swept up cut hair, packed shelves at a supermarket, worked in a petrol station in the middle of nowhere that never got any customers, and they're some of the highlights." She ranged her faraway gaze over the sparsely furnished room. "It's funny how things turn out. What did you want to be when you were a kid?"

I shrugged. Dreams don't mean anything in the real world.

Then she said, "Or did you always want to be a lawn-mowing man?"

I couldn't let that one go. I said, "Actually, I liked writing; I was good at it in school, and everyone believed I'd go places, including my teachers. I thought I'd be a newspaper reporter. Maybe even an editor."

"Yeah? And I wanted to be a ballerina."

She extended her legs and pointed her toes, the skin on her thighs smooth and sprinkled with light-brown freckles. I fixed my gaze at the blank television screen. Rita put her glass on the coffee table and scooched over until her bent leg rested against me. The contact punched my heart into my throat. Then she took one of my hands. Hers were as small as a child's, the fingernails bitten to the quick.

"Please, Ronnie," she whispered, so close now I could smell the wine on her breath, fermented and sharp. "Turn and face me. Please."

I did. She leaned in. I snapped my eyes shut, felt her lips on my mouth. Her tongue pushed insistently past my teeth, and then her arms folded around me, the fingers of one little hand working over my hair and pulling me harder into her kiss, shooting forks of lightning through me, stunning me, my arms limp at my sides, useless, paralysed.

A tapping noise broke her away. She spun her head towards the bolted door that led to the rest of the house, and held up her palm to me in a warning gesture. I sat so still, I even held my breath.

"Ellen?" an elderly female voice said from beyond the door. "Ellen, dear, are you home?"

"Yes, Mrs Foster," Rita said, her voice pitched high and sweet.

As if the palm wasn't enough, Rita frowned at me and shook her head. I nodded that I understood enough to keep quiet.

"Ian and I are leaving for dinner now. We'll be back around nine-thirty. Don't be concerned if you hear noises at about that time, okay, dear?"

"Yes, Mrs Foster. Have a lovely evening."

"Thank you, dear."

The hallway must have had thick carpet, because there weren't any retreating footsteps. Rita, detecting some signal that I didn't, dropped her hand.

"They go out for dinner all the time," she said. "I bet she's an awful cook."

I waited for her to explain. Finally, I said, "Why did she call you Ellen?"

"She thinks my name is Ellen Kennedy."

"And why's that?"

"Because that's what I told her, dummy," she said, and smiled at me with her eyebrows quirked and her head tipped to one side, as if I was the strange one.

3

One night about a week later, I was in the deckchair by my back fence, watching the next-door neighbours, Mr and Mrs Whitmore, through a knothole. Mrs Whitmore was in the kitchen cooking something in a wok, probably a stir-fry, and through the arch behind her, the flicker of the lounge room's TV set, and the lower half of Mr Whitmore's legs, crossed at the ankles and propped on an ottoman. There was only Mrs Whitmore with her plump, young and homely face, and the starry night watching me as I watched her.

"What the fuck are you doing, Ronnie?"

I was on my feet with the deckchair sprawled on its back before I knew it. I never expected Rita would come to my house. The streetlight that shines through the carport silhouetted her face so that I couldn't see her expression. She let out a long, jeering laugh as she walked over. Despite myself, I blushed.

"Oh, I get it," she said. "You're zipped up, but I guess that means you're still waiting for the action to start."

"You've got the wrong idea. There's nothing sick about what I'm doing; it's just human curiosity." My voice rose. "Tell me you've never peeped out your curtain to snoop at the goings-on across the street, or pressed your ear against the wall to hear the argument in the adjoining flat. This is no different."

Rita snorted as if she didn't believe me, and shoved me aside to put her eye at the knothole. Her intake of breath was a sharp whistle.

"She's pregnant," she whispered. "Oh, Ronnie, she's going to have a baby."

Rita's eye went back to the knothole just like mine always did. After a while, she straightened and stared up at me, her widened eyes bright and glinting. "Do you love me, Ronnie? I need to know, right now, yes or no. Do you?"

Casting my gaze down, I nodded. She hugged me, rocking me in her arms from side to side until I stopped shaking, then led me by the hand across the lawn, up the steps and through the back door. I trailed behind until she went to walk into the master bedroom, when I corrected her, and took her into my room, the last door off the hallway to the right.

Straight away, without saying a word, she undressed me.

Her fingers left burning trails on my skin. My strength gone, I sat on the bed while she stripped down, taking off her singlet and cut-off jeans in quick, sure moves. God, she was lovely. I couldn't speak.

She took slow, measured steps towards me, reached out, and stroked her fingers through my hair, sparking electricity across my body. Gently, she held one of my hands and placed it on the firm curve of her breast, the nipple bolt-hard. She guided my hand down her flank until I touched her, and she felt so soft but so hot, hot as a fever, and my heart rolled crazily in my chest.

"Just relax," she whispered, as she cradled my head between her breasts. "Everything's going to be okay, I promise."

I went to turn off the light but she pushed me back onto the mattress.

Afterwards, she lay in my arms. A woman! I could have reached out and stroked her face if I'd felt like it, or put my hand again on other places. It was a miracle. For all the years of my adult life, the only people who'd touched me were the barber, the dentist, the doctor; clients who occasionally shook my hand or clapped my shoulder; strangers who brushed past me on the street, in the supermarket. I spent a few minutes doing the figures in my head: the last person who had hugged me was Mum, precisely 12,852 days ago.

Rita stirred, shifted her head a little on my chest, and said, "Glad I turned up?"

"Very glad. How did you get here?"

"I walked. It's not that far." Then she said, "So where are your parents tonight?"

That threw me, and I even smiled. "In heaven, I suppose. They've been dead a long time; coming up to forty years, in fact."

"Christ almighty, forty fucken *years*? How come you haven't moved into the master bedroom yet?"

"Because that room belongs to my parents."

"Creepy." Rita lifted herself up on an elbow. "It looks like they still live here." She pointed at the dresser and the tallboy, saying, "Did you buy any of this old-fashioned stuff yourself, or was it theirs?"

"No point replacing perfectly good furniture."

"Okay, don't get snippy. So how did they die?"

My mouth opened but nothing came out. Memories of my parents are best viewed with no more than a sideways glimpse. Even though I was an afterthought to their long, dreary marriage, and they didn't particularly love me or even like me that much, my parents were all I had; to be honest, all I have ever had.

"Father went first," I said after a while. "He had a heart attack when I was fifteen. I dropped out of school to take care of Mum. She'd never worked or handled money and she couldn't drive a car. I had to mow lawns to get the bills paid."

"And you've done nothing else but cut grass your whole life?"

That stung, of course. "Well, it's more than just cutting grass," I said, even though it isn't. With every year that had passed, I'd meant to do something about starting my writing career, but other stuff always got in the way, until the point came where I realised that my potential, my ambition, my life, whatever you want to call it, was never going to happen.

Rita said, "What about your mum?"

"A stroke got her three years later."

"Any brothers or sisters?"

"No. Mum and Father were old when they had me. People who didn't know us thought they were my grandparents. Father used to call me the dregs in his coffeepot."

"That's horrible."

"Oh no, he meant it as a joke." But did he? I don't know. Probably not. Actually, it had seemed horrible to me every time he'd said it too, which was often; horrible despite his added wink and chuckle.

"Your old man wouldn't have talked you down like that if I'd been in the picture," Rita said, nuzzling closer and sighing, as if settling down to sleep.

In my bed.

In my arms.

My mind touched upon a thought here and there, lovely thoughts about picnics and sail boating, me and Rita holding hands and smiling at each other so tenderly that strangers passing by couldn't help but point and say, *Look at that couple in love.* And my mind wandered some more and found beautiful thoughts like standing over a cot together, watching our sleeping child. I jumped with panic.

Rita stirred and said in a fuzzy voice, "Ronnie? What's the matter?"

"I didn't use protection."

"Don't worry. Go back to sleep."

She rolled over, hauling most of the sheet with her and wrapping herself in it. All I could see of her was a clump of tangled hair.

"Are you on the Pill?" I said.

"No. Just forget it."

"But Rita, what are we going to do if you're... if we..." My voice was wobbling and reedy and I couldn't make the words sound normal.

"I won't be, okay? Stop flapping, you're keeping me awake."

I regarded the back of her head and listened to my pulse for the longest time. Rita finally turned over.

"What would you do if it turned out I was pregnant?" she said.

"I'd do the right thing. I wouldn't let our child be a bastard. I'd marry you."

Her face was pinched and white. I was afraid that I'd said the wrong thing.

She clutched my hand. "Ronnie, I have to tell you something. Something awful. It might change the way you feel about me."

I put an arm around her and waited.

At last she said, "I can't ever have kids."

I held her. There was only the sound of the two of us breathing. Then she said, "Do you hate me now?"

I kissed the top of her head. "No, of course not."

"But I'm damaged goods."

"We all are, in different ways."

That must have satisfied her because she fell asleep soon after. The next morning, she insisted that two deckchairs had to sit at my back fence.

4

Whenever we went to bed and before Rita would let me touch her, she wanted to talk about nothing else but Mrs Whitmore's baby, and what our lives would be like if the baby belonged to us. I wasn't comfortable about that, but Rita would cling to me with her arms about my neck, begging, "Oh Ronnie, can't we pretend? Just for a little while?"

How could I refuse the woman I loved such a simple request?

Rita liked to fixate on one particular feature of the baby at a time. One night, she said, "Hair or no hair when she's born?"

I lay back on the pillow and gazed at the ceiling to think. Rita snuggled against me. The summer rain tapped on my roof tiles. I had moved into my parents' bedroom a couple of weekends before, Rita helping me shift the furniture, wash the curtains, pack their fusty belongings into boxes, which we stacked in the spare room with the door closed. I had taken to whistling at work. Clients noticed the difference. *My word, look at that spring in your step,* Mrs Caldecott had exclaimed one Wednesday at the retirement village. *You look like a new man.* And I was, I tell you, I *was.*

"Let me see," I said at last. "How about... no hair."

"Not even a bit?"

"Okay, a bit; a single, strawberry-blonde tuft."

Rita laughed. "I reckon her hair will be shoulder-length by her second birthday. It'll grow so fast, I'll have to take her to the hairdresser every six weeks."

151

"Shouldn't girls have long hair anyway?"

Rita sat up so she could better glare at me with big, hectic eyes. "You mean not cut it *ever*? And leave it to grow down to her backside all scraggly with split ends like she's some kind of street urchin?"

"Well no, but I don't think young children like getting their hair cut. Every child I've ever seen in the barber shop is screaming its head off."

"Then we'll give her a chocolate or some kind of treat to keep her quiet."

"Like a bribe?"

"Why not? Adults get rewards for good behaviour, don't they?"

"I suppose."

She folded herself against me and held my hand. "Can you imagine her, Ronnie? The sweetest little thing. And she'll be a daddy's girl, no doubt about it."

"You think?"

"Definitely. You'll be wrapped around Lulu's little finger."

"Lulu?" I said.

"Short for Louise. That would be her name, Louise Kerry Spooner."

"If she was ours," I pointed out, always careful to remind her.

"Yes," she agreed. "If she was ours."

And I wanted it to be true, as much as Rita did, maybe more. That's how it began for me. The little seed that Rita planted took hold and grew like the proverbial Topsy; my most secret, treasured desire I'd given up as unattainable had suddenly taken on life again. Isn't the love of a wife and child every man's dream? By himself, a man doesn't mean a jot to anybody and the world turns whether he's alive or dead, but if you give that man a family, then by God, his life becomes purposeful and important. A man knows he counts for something when he's a husband and a father. And I so much wanted to count for something.

Rita and I concocted wonderful daydreams together. After a while, the daydreams almost seemed like memories. The best one was set on a Queensland beach, and I came back to it time and time again, until I could almost smell the salt, hear the surf:

Rita, in a two-piece bathing suit, yellow with a pattern of red roses, is taking wrapped sandwiches out of the picnic basket. We're sitting on a rug. I've got my hand on Lulu's back, keeping her steady while she fidgets a plastic shovel into the sand, flicking the grains and flapping her other arm in excitement. She's wearing pink bather bottoms with ruffles sewn into the back, pulled over her nappy so she looks about a foot wide, a line of zinc cream across her nose, a little straw hat that keeps tilting off her head. Every now and then, she gives me a grin that's big enough to show her two bottom teeth, which have just cut through. Behind us is our beachfront home with the balcony that leads from the master bedroom to overlook the ocean. And I'm happy. I look at Rita with love in my eyes, and she gives me the same look right back, and together, we smile at Lulu, the centre of our world.

"We'll have a weekend away once a month," Rita said this particular night. We were at her place. It was late and we were sitting up in bed. "We should buy a caravan and go camping. And catch our own fish right out of the river."

"I don't know how to fish," I said.

She had a flushed face and gleaming eyes, her lips swollen from the kissing we'd been doing. I wanted to touch her, yet didn't want her to stop talking. I rolled onto my back. A troupe of daddy longlegs had set up shop in the cornice. For a cleaning lady, Rita wasn't too fussy about her own place; cobwebs, heavy with dust, were strung like haunted-house streamers along her bedroom ceiling, waving in the breeze from the open window.

"Then forget catching fish," she said. "We'll buy a speedboat and teach her to water-ski. Do you know how to water-ski?"

"No. Do you?"

"Fuck it; we'll get her some lessons."

I closed my eyes so the dream could wash over me in brighter colours, but sometimes talking about good things hashes up bad things too. Despite myself, I remembered Christmas, that exhausting, disappointing, wretched day that, as a boy, I'd so learned to dread that even now I keep my head down and just get on with things until it's over.

"What about Christmas?" I said.

"Well, what about it?"

"I don't want it just the three of us."

"Why not?"

In case it calls attention to our misery and we pick each other apart.

Instead, I said, "No-one coming over with presents for her, one big turkey lasting us the whole week, it's not right. Christmas is a family day. We'll visit your relatives for Christmas every year, all right? Or we could alternate; have them at our place one year, and their place the next."

Rita clasped and twisted her hands together, pressing them against her breastbone as if trying to keep something locked inside from coming out. She didn't speak. After so many weeks together, I was used to the peculiar way that she would sometimes disengage from me with no explanation. Minutes passed by. I closed my eyes. Small noises of the night came to my attention; the odd car driving in the distance, a bird flapping around in a tree somewhere, the soft hum of the electric clock.

Rita's voice jarred me out of my half-dream. "Let's see your rellies instead."

"I don't have any," I said. "Mum and Father are dead, remember? And there's no-one else."

She sighed and huffed and flopped about on the bed as if seeking a comfortable spot, but I knew she was agitated. I had enough sense to keep quiet. Rita had never discussed her background before. I didn't know where she was from or where she'd grown up, whether she had siblings, if her parents were alive, the names of friends (if she had any); I didn't even know her birthdate. Nothing. Whenever I had asked her a question about herself, she had fobbed me off with a kiss, a wisecrack, or sometimes the pretence that she hadn't heard me.

After a while, she said, "Just the three of us for Christmas is okay, isn't it?"

And her voice, so timid and small, afraid, as if waiting for the back of a hand, tore me up and made me ashamed.

"Better than okay," I said, and meant it. "Perfect, in fact."

So what if I didn't know the first thing about Rita? She was my woman. I adored her. And besides, I'd spent so many Christmases alone that having anyone at all to share it with thrilled me.

"What about the turkey lasting the whole week?" Rita said.

"I love turkey sandwiches."

"Me too," she said, and kissed me.

5

One Wednesday in late November at the retirement village, I was bagging lawn clippings. Rita had finished cleaning and as soon as I was done, we were going to have lunch together at the dining hall. While talking about our imaginary Queensland beach house, like we always did, Rita said, "How are going to get the baby up there?"

"In the ute with us, of course," I said, like I always did.

"No, I mean *really*." Her uncertain smile revealed just the points of her tiny teeth. "How are we really going to get the Whitmore baby to Queensland?"

I stopped bagging and straightened up. Rita's face was unreadable. I waited for her to say something else but she was waiting for me, so we stood looking at each other in silence.

"We can't," I said finally.

"Why?"

"Because Lulu isn't real, we made her up."

"Okay then," Rita said, "let's pretend. Let's say we wanted to take the Whitmore baby to Queensland with us. How would we do it?"

Her eyes, suddenly wet and fiery, made me look away. I said, "I'm not talking about this."

"Oh, come on, Ronnie, don't get uptight, it's only a game; something to add to the mix." She paced around me. "We follow them into a shopping centre," she continued, "and when Mrs Whitmore's got her back turned, we take off with the pram."

"I don't want to hear you speak this way."

"Or we break in and grab the baby from her cot."

I threw down the rake and the bag. Clippings spilled onto the lawn. Rita's derisive snort took the heat out of me. She picked up the rake and leaned against it, her expression strangely flat.

"Play with me, Ronnie. Make up stories with me."

A wattlebird clattered and clucked in a nearby gum tree. A car sidled along the road and hitched gears as the driver took the speed hump. Sweat trickled from my hairline into my collar. Meanwhile, Rita kept on staring at me and into me, the threat on her face apparent by the tilt of her chin, the narrowing and hardening of her eyes.

I pictured my bed empty of her, more than I could bear, and said, "It's just more stories then?"

She smiled, once again her old self. "Yes, Ronnie. Just more stories."

I nodded, holding out my hand for the rake. She gave it to me. I started on the lawn clippings again.

During lunch and later at Rita's place, for hours and hours we talked of nothing else except stealing Mrs Whitmore's baby. By the time I drove back home, we had the perfect plan.

That night, I was unable to sleep. Lying rigid on my back, as the darkness ticked by towards sunrise, I had to concentrate on breathing slow and easy to keep myself from hyperventilating. The feeling of doom pressed down heavy.

Could I do it? Would I do it?

I didn't know. But one thing I did know for sure, helplessly, was that every decision from then on was out of my hands; that my life and the direction it took was totally up to Rita.

Less than a week later, we were together on my couch, my head resting on Rita's lap while she stroked and smoothed my hair, comforting me while I cried. That afternoon I'd come home from work and checked the knothole. The blue and white striped canvas bag, the one packed with the stuff Mrs Whitmore needed for hospital, the bag that had sat by her kitchen table for the past fortnight, was gone. So was Mrs Whitmore. I'd kept my word and driven straight to Rita's place. She insisted on coming home with me to look through the fence and witness the proof herself.

There was no doubt.

Mrs Whitmore had gone into labour.

"Ronnie, stop crying," Rita said at last, nudging at me until I sat upright on the couch. "You can do this. I know you can. If you help me now, I'll always love you and I'll never leave you. Do you understand?"

I sniffed, hawking up snot, scrubbing at tears with the heels of both hands, and yet nodding anyway. She patted me on the back.

"Then let's get started," she said.

Using my landline phone in the kitchen, she rang around the various hospitals, posing as a concerned friend, until she found the maternity ward that had Mrs Whitmore. My last hope was that the Whitmore baby would be a boy, the only factor that could evaporate Rita's dream of Lulu and halt this demented circus. But Rita called the hospital again at midnight and found out that the baby had been born two minutes before ten p.m.

A girl.

"Lulu is here," Rita said, hanging up, her face glowing. "Oh Ronnie, our little girl is finally here."

I felt too sick to answer.

Rita insisted that I drive her back to her place so that she could prepare straight away. We didn't talk in the ute. What was there to say? Besides, every time I glanced around, Rita's fervid, clenched face and those hands that twisted and squeezed together, as if fighting each other for a chokehold, made me more and more afraid, until I had to keep my eyes latched straight ahead on the road. I should have stopped the ute, refused to go on, told Rita to get out.

But I didn't.

The drive to Rita's place took about ten minutes. During every second of the journey, I hoped to find myself man enough to drive straight into one of the sturdy telegraph poles or gum trees that lined the nature strips every few metres, to press my boot flat against the accelerator and get us up to a hundred or more on a straight run and take the only way out of this nightmare I could think of.

But I didn't.

We pulled up outside her place. She got out of the ute and said, "Don't forget, visiting hours start at two in the afternoon. Come back for me one o'clock sharp."

And I dutifully said that I would, and made my U-turn, flicking on my indicator even though I was the only vehicle in the street.

When I got home to my parents' house, I meandered around for a couple of hours, trying to imagine not living there any more, not seeing the place ever again. I'd been conceived there, and had expected to die there, too. I was to lock up and leave without telling a soul, taking only a suitcase with me, no furniture, no books, no mementoes, not a single keepsake, as if the house, my one and only home, had burned down to its foundations and left nothing behind but ashes. The very thought of it gave me a crushing pain in my chest.

Oh Rita, I kept groaning through my teeth. *Rita.*

That night, I lay on my bed – my real bed, this time, the one in my own room, the last door off the hallway to the right – and stared at the ceiling. An hour or so after the magpies began warbling, I listened to the sounds of the street waking up and coming to life, concentrating, wanting to commit everything to memory. After dragging myself out of bed, I wandered through the house until I felt too miserable to go on. Eating was impossible. I decided to lie down some more and resume staring at the ceiling, and when it was time, I showered, shaved, dressed, and drove to pick up Rita.

She opened the door, and I hardly knew her.

High-heels, tailored pants, a short-sleeved business shirt straining its buttons over a stupendous bustline; her frizzy auburn hair dyed coffee-brown, each strand dovetailed, straight as an arrow, into a bun on the back of her head.

I gaped at this garish vision while she smiled at me.

"Good morning, Mr Spooner," she said, and the voice coming out of that painted scarlet mouth was soft, posh, not Rita's voice at all. "I'm Penelope Teasdale, infant health-care nurse. So very pleased to meet you."

She put out her hand but I didn't take it. Her false nails were deep, dark red like her lips, red as blood, red as guts.

"What have you done?" I said, stammering. "You're going to stand out in that get-up."

"Yep, like dog's balls," she said, this time in her usual strapping tone. "And that's the whole point, Ronnie. Think for a second: when the shit hits, they'll be looking for a brunette with big boobs, and that's not me."

6

I drove us to the hospital and parked near the entrance to the maternity wing. At two in the afternoon, the car park was nearly full. The sun roasted a wavering heat haze off the rows of vehicles spread out around us. I killed the ute's engine and turned to Rita with a frown, trying to find a way to ask her to stop such silliness, but Rita immediately leapt from the ute and started clip-clopping in her towering heels towards the hospital entrance. The dark bun on the back of her head bobbed as she weaved between parked cars. Then the double doors of the building swallowed her up, and she was gone.

That particular section of the hospital has sixteen front windows. I know this because I had a lot of time to count them, over and over, forwards and backwards, right to left, left to right, up and down, down and up, odds and evens, diagonally, and so on, in countless mathematical patterns. For the next quarter hour I counted, while my eyes watered and stung. The ute rolled beneath me in wave after queasy wave, but I think that's just a trick of the brain when you haven't slept in a while.

Finally, I spotted Rita again, and could shut my eyes. An after-image of sixteen windows wobbled against the red-black of my lids. I heard her open the passenger door of the ute and get in.

"The maternal and child health-care nurse had already seen her. Shit, I had to tell her I was from the regional branch; fuck knows if there's any such thing, but ah well, she's not likely to check. She's going home Friday morning. Mr Whitmore is still on leave for the next two weeks. That means we'll have to do it when he's out of the house, but don't worry, I'll only need a few minutes."

I opened my eyes. "Why don't you wait until he's back at work?"

"So Lulu bonds with Mrs Whitmore instead of me?" she demanded, as if the baby was a freshly hatched bird, chirping for something – anything – upon which to imprint its notion of mother. I decided not to answer.

Rita pulled the socks out of her bra, tossed them into the foot well, and continued, "What am I going to do about this hair? I can't have the Fosters seeing it. Maybe I'll stay at your place from now on."

When we got home, she wanted to celebrate. All I had was light beer. She poured a couple of glasses and ended up drinking them both herself – I couldn't stomach any. Then she sent me on a shopping expedition four suburbs away, to buy supplies for Lulu.

Oh, I'd imagined a few shelves of products, but nothing like this.

As I headed down the supermarket's baby aisle with a basket, I was confronted by hundreds of tins, jars, bottles, boxes and bags of more items than an infant could surely ever use in a lifetime, stretching from one end of that long, long aisle to the other; a dozen brands for each item, different sizes and types and prices; and packaging listing complicated categories such as age, weight, sex and height, or bewildering options that didn't mean anything to me, such as gluten-free, lactose-free, organic, hypoallergenic; and so on, and on and on. Astonishing. Suddenly, fatherhood sounded like a frightening morass.

My meagre shopping list fitted on a sticky-note – shampoo, soap, baby wipes, barrier cream, talcum powder, disposable nappies, bottles, formula powder, dummies, bibs, singlets, grow suits – but it took me over two agonising hours to complete. Perspiring through my clothes, I worried about store detectives watching me on hidden video monitors, getting suspicious (who is this dithering pervert?), expecting a heavy hand to grip my shoulder. But nothing happened.

At the checkout, I paid for my purchases and left. No-one followed me into the car park. Unmolested, I drove away, my foot quivering on the pedals.

I was still shaking when I got home. Rita didn't bother to check my purchases. I put everything in the spare room right next to the boxes that held my parents' belongings, the bland faces of each carton somehow managing to stare accusingly at me.

After dinner, which I couldn't eat, I drove Rita home one last time so she could pick up her things. I offered to help her, but she insisted I wait in the ute.

She returned inside five minutes.

The only thing she carried was her giant hessian bag, which was bulging only a little more than usual. She slammed the ute door and fussed with her seatbelt while I stared at the solitary bag.

"That's it?" I said.

"Yep, let's go."

"That's everything you own?" I said. "In the whole world?"

"Come on, Ronnie, get moving."

I put the ute into gear and steered from the kerb. Rita didn't give the Foster place another glance. She sat back in the seat, thumbed her nose and gazed out the window, humming, as if pulling up stakes and leaving everything behind was easy, a trifling finger-snap. And for the first time, it occurred to me that, perhaps, leaving me behind would be just as easy for her, given the right circumstances, and my guts roiled around.

Did Rita love me? Or was she using me? While driving her back to my house that night, having faith in her love was, quite frankly, the only thing that kept me going, that kept my heart beating, the breath dragging in and out of my chest. My faith in her was all I had.

The Whitmore house was full of visitors that weekend. We took turns at the knothole, waiting for our opportunity, which we didn't get. Rita spent the two days pacing, gnawing at her bottom lip with her sharp little incisors, staring at me with glazed eyes whenever she wasn't at the knothole with her shoulders hunched, her hands on the fence, fingers splayed and clawed stiff against the palings. I watched her from the window and bit at my nails.

First thing Monday morning, I called my customers and told them I was ill. That's the only time I've ever pulled a sickie, and I found it hard to keep my thoughts together. At about lunchtime, during Rita's watch at the fence, I drove to the milk bar and got another newspaper. I'd bought every one since Mrs Whitmore's baby was born. When I got home, I spread the paper on the kitchen table and turned to the birth notices in the classified section. There it was:

Jennifer and Colin Whitmore are thrilled to announce the safe arrival of Abby Rose, 7lb 8oz at 9.58pm, December 16th. Thanks to Dr Chang and the midwifery staff...

The rest blurred in front of my eyes. I sat down, unable to trust my legs to hold me up.

Abby.

Little Abby Rose Whitmore.

It seemed important so I pushed myself to my feet and went out and told Rita. She didn't move her eye from the knothole.

Monday felt about a week long. Mr Whitmore still hadn't left the house. I watched hours of TV. The weather forecast was clear and sunny; for a change of pace, I packed our bags and boxes into the open tray of my ute. Later, I took my turn at the knothole. Later still, when it was turning dark and I was off-duty, numb and drained, once again slumped in front of the TV, the back door slammed open, startling me. Rita shouldered her way to the centre of the lounge room and stood for a moment, panting, her face tensed, hot flushes stamped on both cheeks.

I leapt from the couch.

And froze.

This is what happens when you can't say no, I realised. This is what happens when you'll do anything, anything at all, to keep someone you love happy.

Rita scrabbled out of her singlet and shorts and into the Penelope Teasdale outfit that had been lying for days on the seat of a kitchen chair. She glared while she zipped and buttoned, but I couldn't move.

"Come on, Ronnie," she said. "Get cracking, will you? Jesus."

Stuporous, I shambled after her into the backyard. Since the rails are on the Whitmore side of the fence, I had to lift Rita onto the barbecue so that she was high enough to clamber over. In her haste, one of her feet slid off the top railing. For a dizzying moment, I thought she was going to fall and maybe break a leg, which meant this whole crazy thing would be called off and I could go back to mowing lawns the very next day, but she didn't fall. Instead, her feet found every rail on the descent. Then she was in the Whitmore backyard, no doubt sprinting as quickly as her high-heels would let her through the carport and around to the Whitmore front door.

Time to fit the baby capsule into the ute.

I took a step from the fence. My foot mashed against the ground. Surprised, I took another step and almost collapsed. My bones had turned to mush. Making my way over the lawn felt like crossing a tar pit.

I grabbed the baby capsule out of the carport and wrestled open one of the rear doors on my dual-cab ute. By now, it was getting dark and I wanted to keep it that way, so I didn't switch on the outside light. I'd figured the job would take me three or four minutes, at the most.

I was wrong. It turns out that a baby capsule is an infernally complicated contraption with harnesses and hooks, tethers, buckles, and mystifying little slots and grooves; accompanied by a ten-page instruction manual crammed with scores of dire warnings flagged in red type.

Adrenaline churned my stomach. I'd wanted to install the capsule as soon as we'd got the restraining bolt mounted in the ute, but Rita had cautioned that it would look suspicious if a single man with no children took to driving an empty baby capsule around. And she was right, of course. I'd agreed to wait 'til the plan was in motion. I slogged at the capsule fittings with trembling fingers, sweat coursing down my face, cursing, ears straining for the barest sound of Rita's voice. God forbid, was she already clutching Lulu and waiting for me by the fence?

Mr Dabrowski, my neighbour from directly across the road, must have been wearing his crepe-soled gardening shoes. I didn't hear him walk up my driveway until it was too late.

7

"Need a hand?"

My breath snagged. I turned my head and looked at Mr Dabrowski, not two feet away. The tip of his cigarette flared red as he took a drag.

"Looks like you're having some problems, Ron," he said.

I had no choice but to get out of the ute. The tiny muscles around my mouth started shivering. "No, I'm fine, Mr Dabrowski, thank you. Mild night, isn't it?"

"Yep." He waved his cigarette towards the open door of the ute. "Aw, those things can be a right bitch to install."

I followed his gaze. We both looked at the baby capsule for a while.

He continued, "I'm putting the mongrels in and out of cars all the time. Seven grandkids. Why didn't you give me a hoi? I'd be happy to put it in for you. There's a knack, you see. Upper anchorage strap. Get that right and you're laughing. What do you need it for?"

A pulse started thumping deep in my guts. "My sister's car has broken down. She needs me to give her and the baby a lift home."

As soon as I said it, I broke out in hot panic. God, what a pinheaded, dumb mistake; Mr Dabrowski has lived across the road from us since before I was born, and knows I'm an only child.

"Actually, she's my friend," I added, "but I think of her as a sister. Well, anyway, thanks for dropping by."

"Going on a trip?"

In full view in the back of the ute, right there in the open tray, sat my suitcase, and the grocery bags and boxes that contained the baby products. My weight shifted from one foot to the other, compulsively, and I couldn't stop. Rita was waiting at the fence, I was sure of it, and she would be scared and getting ready to bellow my name.

"Yes, I'll be away for a few days," I said. "My friend lives in Bendigo."

"Bendigo?" Mr Dabrowski said, and laughed, a rumbling wheeze. "Come off it, Ron. She's going to wait in her broken-down car with her bub for two hours until you get there?"

Eventually, I said, "No, that's another friend of mine. I'm helping one first, just up the road, the friend with the broken-down car. Next I'm going to visit the other one, the one who lives in Bendigo. Two separate friends."

"Uh huh," he said, smiling, but with only one side of his mouth, which made me nervous. "Sounds like they're keeping you busy. Leaving for Bendigo tonight?"

"That's right."

"Pretty late for a long drive."

I didn't say anything.

He took a slow puff of his cigarette. "Well, Ron," he said, "I was talking to Mr Norris this morning, and he's under the impression you're cutting out that dead hydrangea for him tomorrow afternoon."

"That would be next week."

"No, he definitely said tomorrow."

"Then he's mistaken."

Mr Dabrowski dropped the butt and ground it underfoot. Watching me, nodding sagely, as if everything was slowly but surely becoming clear to him, he pulled out a packet of cigarettes from the pocket of his shorts and lit another smoke with his disposable lighter. My heart began to skip beats here and there.

"That's my telephone, I have to go," I said, another lame and obvious lie, but the best I could do, and sprinted across the lawn to the back door.

I flung myself into the lounge room and watched him through a chink in the curtains. Mr Dabrowski didn't leave. Instead, he took long drags of his smoke while he leaned his buffalo body to one side and peered through the cab. Another minute passed, one slow and excruciating second after another. Once the cigarette was down to the stub, he let it fall from his hand to the driveway, hitched up his shorts, eased his bulk face-first into the back seat of the ute, one fat knee at a time, and started fiddling with the baby capsule.

I ran to the window on the other side of the lounge room and gaped at the fence, praying for x-ray vision. Then I ran back to watch Mr Dabrowski. He was still in the ute. My eyes bored holes in his back. The fat quivered through his tight polo shirt while he worked his arms. I waited for Rita's yelling to start. I bit my thumb and kept on biting, tasting blood.

At last, Mr Dabrowski heaved himself out of the ute.

For a moment, he seemed to be heading towards the back door of my house; sweet relief, he changed his mind, walking instead down my driveway and out of sight, presumably towards his own house. As soon as he was gone, I tore to the fence.

"Rita, are you there?" I hissed.

"Jesus, what the *fuck* is going on?"

"We have to call it off. Mr Dabrowski was here. He's seen everything."

"It's too late for that. Take the baby."

"Put her back, please. We can't go through with it."

Her voice spat frantically, "Ronnie, he's in the driveway."

With a gasp, I spun around, expecting to see Mr Dabrowski standing right on my heels. No-one was there.

"Didn't you hear me?" she said. "He's in the driveway. Mr Whitmore's in the fucken *driveway.*"

An object whirled over the fence and thumped into my lawn without a single bounce, heavy as a shot put. For one crazed instant, I thought it was Lulu, until I recognised the shape as Rita's faux-leather handbag. Rita's high heels scrabbled and kicked into the railings as she started her climb.

"Ronnie, help me, for Christ's sake."

My shin barked on the metal edge of the barbecue lid; then I was standing up and leaning over the fence at Rita's sharp, determined face. She was scaling the rails with one hand, clutching a wrapped bundle in the other. Darkness sprang across the Whitmore backyard; Mr Whitmore must have switched off his car headlights. Plump, homely Mrs Whitmore was probably already out the front door and running across the porch to tell him the ghastly news through wracking sobs. Dear God, she more than likely had her cordless phone with the police on the line.

"Take her," Rita ordered. "Take Lulu for me."

I reached down. My hands closed around the bundle, around our baby. Despite the madness going on, I still paused to marvel – how tiny, how light – and then I tucked her under one arm.

Rita was at the top of the fence with a leg dangled over. I grabbed Rita about the waist with my other arm, hauled, and set her down on the barbecue next to me. She pushed out of my grasp, leapt to the ground, made a beeline to the handbag, snatched it up and sprinted to the ute. She didn't look back. With a jolt, I imagined her driving off without me. Before I could stop myself, I had already slapped at my pocket with my free hand, feeling the set of car keys, reassuring myself that she couldn't leave me behind even if she tried.

I slid off the barbecue and found my legs had turned to mush again. I waded through the lawn like I was sinking into the earth. I must have been moving faster than I thought, however, because the bundle in my arms jerked and jounced so hard that I had to hug it with both arms.

"Put her in the capsule," Rita said, her heels ringing on the concrete as she darted to the front passenger side of the ute.

"There's no time," I said. "Hold her in your lap."

Mr Dabrowski's porch light was on. I could make out his scrappy parade of grafted rose bushes lining the front of his lawn. But where was Mr Dabrowski?

Rita flung open the passenger door. "No way. It's Christmas holidays; booze buses and speed traps are everywhere, on every single road out of here. Put her in the capsule now." She got in the ute and shut the door.

I did as I was told. My first sight of the baby repulsed me. The face, red and scrunched, had a scaly rash across both cheeks, and yellow crusts clotted the stumpy eyelashes. This creature looked like an ugly old gnome in miniature. It wasn't my Lulu at all; I didn't want to touch it, didn't want anything to do with it.

"Hurry up," Rita yelled.

I fought with the straps of the capsule. The baby opened its pink, slimy mouth and made grumbling, grizzling noises. The tiny fists worked their way out of the blanket, and began flailing around in front of the scowling face.

My jaw clenched hard enough to hurt my teeth. "Don't cry," I whispered. "Please, please, don't cry."

"Oh shit," Rita breathed. "Is that him?"

Rita was so very still, her dead-ahead gaze so fixed through the windscreen, that time seemed to crack and stop for a terrible moment. I twisted around in the seat. Mr Dabrowski was standing in his front yard directly opposite my driveway, and looking right at us, the red dot of his cigarette flaring like a beacon in the twilight. The beacon started to bob up and down, rapidly getting closer.

"Hurry up, Ronnie. He's coming."

The last strap on the baby capsule clicked into the clasp. I vaulted from the back seat, slammed the door and threw myself behind the steering wheel. Striding briskly and purposefully towards us, Mr Dabrowski had just reached the nature strip outside my house when Mr Whitmore let out a scream.

8

That keening wail sliced through every window, door crack and roof tile of the Whitmore house, and knifed across the neighbourhood louder than any other sound I've ever heard in my life. Rita and I flinched in our seats. Mr Dabrowski snapped to attention. The air itself seemed to pause in alarm. The scream stopped long enough for a breath to be drawn, then it started again, the kind of full-throated shrieking you imagine a man would make if a shark hit him.

I started the engine. My feet stammered on the pedals. Rita must have thought I was about ready to stall the ute because she smacked the side of my head with her open hand and barked out, "Go. *Go now*."

The baby let out a howling yell and began to cry. Her father's tormented scream stopped and started again. My mind ripped, tearing away from me, and I thought, numbly, I must be going into shock. Even so, I couldn't take my eyes off Mr Dabrowski. Outside lights flicked on at number sixteen, number fourteen and next door at the Bennings. Mr Whitmore was drawing out the whole street.

Mr Dabrowski took a couple of strides closer, flushing panic back into me; I stamped the accelerator and clipped the letterbox on the way out of the driveway. Mr Dabrowski took an involuntary backward leap, as if he expected me to thump right over the top of him. I ploughed the ute up the street. Mr Dabrowski dashed onto the road and stared after us, growing smaller in my rear-view mirror. I slowed the ute to a crawl. Mr Dabrowski turned toward the screaming with his beefy body held still and his nose angled into the air, looking like one of those pointer dogs that sees a duck flail down into the scrub somewhere, alerting the hunter to where the prey has fallen.

There was no traffic in these residential streets. I could have turned at the next intersection straight away. Instead, I idled at the Give Way sign with the indicator ticking, and watched the rear-view mirror.

Mr Dabrowski jogged across the road, gesturing with an arm wave for Mrs Green and her son Scotty to follow him. I could see old Mr Thatcher on his front step, and he must have been shouting something at them because he circled his cane in the air, and Mr Dabrowski wheeled around as if shouting something back. The baby squalled on and on.

"We did it. Fuck, we really *did* it." Rita broke into giggles that sounded loose and edgy, as if they could turn into hysterics. She clamped a hand on my knee, hard enough to hurt. "We're a family now, aren't we Ronnie? Come on, what are you waiting for? Get your family out of here."

I put the ute in gear. My street swung out of the rear-view mirror and disappeared. Sudden grief choked me. I had nothing but a suitcase. My brand new life – my big open future – consisted of shirts, shorts, underpants and shaving gear.

In less than a minute, I pulled up at the intersection with the main road. Our plan was to head north and drive for as long as we could; after an overnight stay at a motel in whichever place we ended up, we'd get on the Hume and take the Pacific Highway to Queensland. But the line of headlights both ways on this main road wouldn't stop. We were foiled already, trapped within my housing estate. Helpless, I hung onto the steering wheel and waited for a space to open up.

The baby cried. The traffic flowed. I checked the rear-view mirror. Any second now, surely, there'd be a posse of my lifelong neighbours running up to the ute, armed with shovels and secateurs, baying for me.

"We should have put her back," I said. "Mr Dabrowski will know it was us."

"Get going, get moving."

"How?"

"Push your way out."

"There's no break."

Rita leaned her hand on the horn. "Edge in, for Christ's sake."

I lurched the ute forward into the lane. A courier van braked hard and tipped onto its front wheels. Hot and flushed, I kangaroo-hopped the ute with quaking feet. A Statesman swerved onto the shoulder to avoid hitting me. Rita's hand was still on the horn. Answering blasts clamoured from vehicles in both lanes. The baby screamed blue murder. I was asphyxiating in noise.

I slapped Rita's hand away from the horn. She gave me a stony look then leaned over to wind an arm around my neck and stab her tongue into my ear. I pulled away, which made her laugh.

"I'm a mother now," she said, momentarily digging her hand between my thighs. "Do you still find me sexy?"

I shuttled the ute forward until we merged into the stream of traffic on the main road. The man behind me in the Statesman gave me the finger. We started moving. The traffic light ahead turned yellow.

"Gun it, go through it," Rita said.

Of course I obeyed, despite the red light camera at the intersection. What did an infringement notice matter to me now? What did anything matter?

Finally, I could get the ute to a decent speed. We drove, not speaking, the baby yowling. A booze bus sat on the other side of the road, lights blinking. Two police officers were walking the lane and putting out traffic cones to set up the station. I prayed there'd be no breath-testing along our route. I hadn't been drinking, of course, but an officer would only have to take one look at my clammy face and guilty eyes and know straight away to draw his gun. The thought made me tremble.

"Why didn't you return the baby?" I said.

Rita switched on the radio and started humming along to whatever song was playing, tapping her fingers on her handbag to keep the beat, like we were on a leisurely Sunday drive. The crying stopped, abruptly, as if cut off. We both turned in alarm. The baby appeared to be asleep, with one tiny set of knuckles locked into its suckling mouth.

"Ah, peace at last," Rita said, and began humming again.

My mobile phone rang. Without daring to check caller ID, I switched it off. Then I bit my lips and drove. As we neared the bridge that runs over the creek, Rita told me to pull over. I obeyed. She got of the ute, took something from her Penelope Teasdale handbag, and tossed whatever it was over the railing.

"What did you throw away?" I said, as she got back in and slammed the door.

"Oh, not much; just a little token that helps me say goodbye to Rita McNaughton."

"Goodbye?"

"That's right." She clipped her seatbelt and gestured for me to start driving again. "I'm thinking of calling myself Melanie Andrews."

"Melanie Andrews?"

"It sounds pretty. Like it?"

"Sorry, I don't think I understand," I said, even as the memory of Rita's landlady calling her Ellen Kennedy rushed at me like a terrible harbinger.

Rita said, "We're supposed to be married, so you've got to be Andrews too. What kind of first name takes your fancy?"

"I've got to have a different name?"

"Well, shit yeah, dummy."

That flabbergasted me. I actually stuttered for a few seconds, unable to get the words out. "How on earth are we are going to live if I can't use my real name any more? What about my drivers licence, credit cards, bank accounts?"

"We'll be fine."

"Fine? How will we be fine? What are we going to do? Steal identities from dead people?"

"Hah. Nothing that ridiculous."

My head felt unnaturally light and spacey. "God, I'm a fugitive."

Rita laughed. "Oh Frank, don't be such a drama queen."

"Frank?"

"Frank Andrews. That's you."

"Rita, I can't –"

"Nuh-uh, *Melanie*," she said. "The name's Melanie from now on. It's important to remember that, okay? Very, very important."

As if to give me a massage, she clamped her hand onto the back of my neck. Instead of caressing, however, the strong little fingers dug in hard.

9

About an hour went by. For most of that time, we'd been driving through unsavoury neighbourhoods: the sort without trees or parks; where grimy factories with barbed-wire fences and graffiti are located directly across the road from sagging fibro-cement houses, front yards full of rubbish or broken car bodies; where groups of people lounge together without purpose in the shadows of street corners, drinking from bottles, faces hidden by jacket-hoods or caps. You wouldn't want your vehicle to break down in areas like that.

Traffic slowed to a crawl as we approached another strip shopping centre. Despite the giant tinsel Christmas bells that hung from telegraph poles, the place didn't look cheery. Many of the shops had newspaper sheets and faded 'To Let' signs stuck on the windows. Even so, the strip had plenty of people walking the broken footpaths doing their late-night Christmas shopping.

The traffic came to a complete stop at a pedestrian crossing. Some kind of foreign music thumped out of a nearby pawn store. I locked the ute doors.

Rita sniggered, pointed with her thumb, and said, "Jeez, would you take a look at that old dero? You'd reckon they could've found someone better than that."

On our side of the street, next to the swing doors of a department store, a shabby Santa Claus was clanging a tarnished bell and yelling, "Ho, ho, ho," to the fed-up shoppers pushing past him. The Santa suit hung off his bony frame.

I shuddered with revulsion. I've never liked Santa Claus.

Some children are scared of clowns, and everyone understands that fear: it's those larger-than-life features; the unnaturally pale skin; the red, gaping mouth that looks ready to take a bite out of you. I'm not particularly fond of clowns, either. But when I was little, my greatest fear was Santa Claus. No-one, least of all my parents, could understand or sympathise.

To me, he was an omniscient monster that could somehow live forever, survive the North Pole, spy on me throughout the year without detection, and break into my house while I slept. One of my first memories of Santa involves a photo shoot, probably at a local shopping plaza. Mum put me on Santa's lap. The fake beard frightened the daylights out of me. If his beard was fake, my young mind reasoned, then other portions of Santa's body must be fake too. Like some kind of freakishly alive Mr Potato Head, I imagined that other parts of Santa's body – his teeth, his nose, his eyeballs – could also be pulled away. Of course, these horrifying thoughts led to me screaming, and then to Mum smacking me because I'd embarrassed her in front of strangers.

As I grew up, I learned to control my nerves. The most I feel when I'm around a person dressed up as Santa Claus is mild unease. But at that moment, strung out with anxiety, a kidnapped newborn in the back of my ute, while stuck at the red light of a pedestrian crossing in a slummy, unsafe neighbourhood, I stared at this particular Santa, and quailed. He wore his fake beard tucked under his jaw rather than against his chin. I was two years old again. If he grabs at his nose, I found myself thinking, it will come off in his hand.

Rita, laughing, shouted through her open window, "Hey, Father Christmas, you ought to be in rehab."

Santa, only a few feet away, turned to us. Perhaps he saw the fear in my eyes and it amused him, because he smiled at me. I felt suffocated. Santa clanged his bell. Then, in a gesture that raised the hairs on the back of my neck, he lifted his free arm high into the air and started rolling it from side to side, straight from the shoulder, waving at me as if I was far from shore.

"Good will to all men," he called. "Even you."

I nodded. He lowered his waving arm and held it out towards me, pointing his forefinger as if sighting along a rifle. *Bang.*

I started to cry.

Rita slapped me on the leg. "What the hell? What the fuck is wrong with you?"

Santa hobbled over and leaned down to the open window, one hand on the sill. "Having a hard time, mate?" he said. One of his front teeth was gone, just like in my nightmares of Mr Potato-Head Santa, and I recoiled in my seat, the sobs gagging in my throat.

"Piss off, you dirty drunk," Rita said, "or I'll stab you in the fucken eyes."

He laughed, pushing away from the ute.

"What a freak," Rita said, closing the window.

Santa continued ringing his bell and performing to the shoppers coming in and out of the department store. I couldn't look away from him in case he sneaked up on me unawares.

"Light's green, let's go," Rita said, slapping me again. "And for God's sake, stop crying."

The line of traffic in front began to pull away. Car horns sounded behind us. A harsh male voice hollered from somewhere, *Get a move on, dickhead.* My foot stayed frozen on the brake.

Rita grabbed my collar and shook me. "What are you waiting for?" she said. "Get going."

I took one last look at Santa. He gave me a snappy salute. My foot jammed onto the accelerator. The ute skidded forward. I was hyperventilating, getting dizzy, blinking my eyes repeatedly to clear the encroaching grey fog.

"Are you okay?" Rita said, gently this time. "You're so pale. God, you're not gonna faint, are you?"

"Yes. I have to stop and rest."

"Stop? You mean stop driving? You're kidding me. Right now?"

"Now."

"But we've only started. How long will it take to hit Queensland if we pull over every hour and a quarter?"

On the other side of the upcoming intersection sat a motel, its tattered neon and plywood sign proclaiming vacancies and cheap rates. I swung the ute through the open iron gate and along the gravel driveway.

Rita huffed. "Oh, you mean stop for the *night*? Aw, hell."

The motel was on a skinny rectangular block. The double-storey terraces of cream brick ran down one long side of the rectangle, with a scrappy hedgerow and dumpsters on the other. I pulled up outside reception and engaged the handbrake, leaving the motor running. For a few moments, we sat in the ute in silence. A white-blonde head popped up from behind the reception desk. A pair of dark-rimmed spectacles examined us.

"All right," Rita said. "We'll book in, if that's what you have to do."

I nodded gratefully and took one of her hands. She pulled it from my grasp.

"And for Christ's sake," she said, "let me do the talking."

10

I woke up. My eyes stayed shut. I ached worse than I ever have. A pillow pushed against my cheek; therefore, I reasoned, I must be on a bed. The mattress was spongy and soft. I wriggled my toes, and my boots were still on; shifting, I felt my clothes, belt, collar. Where was I? A sense of dread pulled me up. I was lying down in a strange place fully dressed; to think beyond that would be trouble, so I stopped thinking altogether and just lay there.

Rita's voice: "I know you're awake."

There was a moment of suspension, of ignorance, then the sordid mess ran over me and I groaned through my teeth. I wanted to die. No, more than that – I wished I'd never been born.

"Look at me, Ronnie."

She was slouched in a wing chair, her legs crossed and slung over one of the arms, her uppermost foot waggling back and forth. The glow from the bedside lamp caught and winked on her toe ring. The Penelope Teasdale outfit was gone. Instead, she wore one of my shirts buttoned low on her chest, and nothing else.

My joints creaked as I sat up, suddenly an old man. "What time is it?"

"Nearly midnight."

I surveyed the motel room: a cheap jumble of plywood, vinyl, and acrylic; a wall-mounted bench with a kettle and teacups, a television, a freestanding wardrobe, two single beds separated by bedside tables. The place stunk of lemon detergent and dust, with a disagreeable undertone of various body odours, as if every previous occupant had left behind a scent-phantom. Thoughts of my own home started an aching pang in my guts.

"Where's the baby?" I said.

"Bathed, fed, and asleep, no thanks to you. I've got her in the shower stall on a pillow. You forgot to get a portable cot."

"You didn't write it on the list."

Her foot kept swinging, the toe ring kept winking, and she kept looking at me, poker-faced. "I thought we were in this thing together."

"Of course we are."

"I thought you loved me."

"Rita, I do love you. Honestly, I do."

"Then why are you carrying on like this? You've got everything you've ever wanted."

Tears crowded my eyes and closed my throat. "Oh, Rita," I whispered. "We've done an awful, awful thing."

Her foot stopped swinging. At first, I thought I'd offended her. Then she uncrossed her legs and, knees together, placed her bare feet on the floor. Very slowly, knowingly, gazing at me intently while I stared at her, she worked her toes into the threadbare nap of the carpet and began to walk her feet out wider and wider, spreading her thighs. I stopped crying. When she bunched up the shirt onto the firm flatness of her belly, exposing herself completely to me, I stopped breathing.

"Undress," she said.

And I struggled out of my clothes, fumbling with buttons, baffled by zips. At last, I stood naked, and she held out her hand.

"Now come over here with that thing," she said, "and I'll make you feel better."

Later, spent, I fell back onto one of the single beds and closed my eyes for a moment. When I opened them again, a huge gum tree filled the motel room. Branches reached across the ceiling and speared into the walls. I turned my head to remark upon this to Rita; she was gone. A cracking sound pulled my attention back to the tree. Something was working its way out of the trunk.

The wood split. Out came a hand, then a whole arm. Suddenly, Mrs Whitmore's head and shoulders were squirming out of the tree. She was trying to climb out, except her hips were stuck. She wore a bikini, or maybe bra and panties, the skin on her torso stiff and yellow like raw pork rind. As I watched her struggling, black and purple bruises started flowering over her. The crackling skin must have been brittle; as she frantically butted her hips against the bark, striving to free her legs, shavings of flesh crumbled and flaked off. The purple-black mottle spread and joined up until she looked burnt to a crisp.

My eyes wouldn't close. I threw an arm over my face. The scrabbling noises stopped. I lowered my arm. The tree and Mrs Whitmore were gone. There was just Rita standing with her back to me.

"Jesus," I gasped. "Rita, I had the most horrible nightmare."

She whirled around without moving her legs, as if on a turntable, holding the long handle of a shovel in both hands. The blood on her – not her own, someone else's – gleamed shiny-black from head to toe, great gouts of it, as if thrown from a bucket. There was even blood smeared around her mouth, reminding me, with horror, of the grease stains you get from eating fried chicken. I knew what was coming. Nevertheless, I couldn't move. She hoisted the handle over her shoulder, brandishing it like you would a baseball bat. The blade whistled through the air. Right before impact, I lurched awake, filmed in sweat.

I sat up, not sure it I was still dreaming. The red glow of the digital alarm clock showed 4.18 a.m. The street light shining around the margins of the curtain cast soft shadows about the room. Rita lay in her bed with her back to me, snoring, the sheet up to her ear. I went over, swaying on unsteady legs as if on a plane flying through chop. She was curled up with both hands tucked under her cheek, her lower lip sucked partway into her mouth. It was like looking upon a sleeping child.

I opened the bathroom door. The baby was a dark blur through the dimpled-glass panels of the shower recess. I couldn't bring myself to go any closer.

Quietly, I took Rita's giant hessian bag from her bedside and retreated to the bathroom, shutting the door ever so gently behind me, fearing that a click of the latch might wake her or the baby. The door closed without sound. I propped the bag on the edge of the sink, pulled out the lighted shaving mirror on its arm, and by its dim glow, rifled through Rita's belongings, searching for answers.

It was a frustrating array of commonplace items: shorts, singlets, underwear, hairbrush, toiletries bag, makeup purse, assorted pens, a spiral-bound notebook with most of the pages torn out, a box of mints, sunglasses, sun block, a travel pack of facial tissues, hand cream, a pair of sandals, a pocket knife, and then, jarringly, two unopened packets of surgical latex gloves. I pondered on the gloves for a time, and kept digging. No mobile phone, address book, or diary planner. Her wallet, brown leather with a built-in coin purse, sat at the very bottom of the hessian bag, heavy as a billiard ball. Inside it, some folded money and plenty of change, but no credit cards, identification, or personal information of any sort. Stymied, close to tears, in my final, desperate scrutiny, I discovered a zippered compartment hidden inside the coin purse; within it, eureka, part of a colour photograph cut down with scissors to the size of a matchbox.

I held the photograph to the mirror's light bulb. The sliver revealed the face of a girl of about two years of age, with a short cap of fine, red hair. Perhaps this was a snapshot of Rita's baby, I surmised, the real Lulu, the daughter Rita may have lost or had taken from her in some way, the missing baby she couldn't stop looking for and felt compelled to replace. A reasonable theory.

Then I noticed the child's grim face, her clenched smile. Could it be a photograph of Rita herself? In the background were the shelves of a colonial-style bureau, loaded with fussy china plates and figurines; the type of bureau that has cupboards at the bottom, which meant that someone, presumably an adult, perhaps her mother or father, must be holding that little girl on their hip for the photographer. I leaned closer to the snippet of film. The child had green eyes.

Was it Rita?

Yes, I decided. And this was the only memento of her life that she permitted herself; the family, whoever they were and whatever they had done to her, carefully and deliberately excised. For a moment, I wanted to hold her, and peck little kisses across her eyelids, nose and cheeks, until I remembered the awful thing that we had done on her instigation. Then I felt sick again.

I crept back to Rita's bedside, returning the hessian bag. When I spoke, my voice sounded odd to my own ears, the words muffled and far away. I said, "How did you manage to take the baby from her?"

The snoring stopped. Rita's body tensed under the sheet.

I continued, "Mr Whitmore was screaming, but not Mrs Whitmore. Why wasn't she screaming?"

Rita turned over, slow and deliberate, and contemplated me for a long moment. "Ronnie. It's late. You're tired. Go to sleep." She rolled over again, wrenching up the sheet to her ear.

"And another thing," I said. "Why aren't you calling me

Frank? I haven't been calling you Melanie either, and for some reason that's not bothering you."

"Let's worry about that crap tomorrow. For now, just shut the fuck up."

Bewildered, I climbed into my single bed. The linen felt rough against my skin. The pillow smelled of wet dog. I took a breath and tried to relax. Sleep wouldn't come. I lay on my back with Rita's snoring for company, waiting for the world to come into focus, listening to the traffic noises start up, watching the shadows in the room gradually lighten.

The baby began to cry. Rita, tousle-headed and naked, shambled out of bed and shuffled into the bathroom, closing the door behind her. It was 6.03 a.m. I steeled myself for whatever was to come.

11

Rita, dressed in her customary shorts and top, sat cross-legged on the bed, giving the baby a bottle and me my instructions.

"The old bag's already been paid for the room," she said, "so don't worry, go ahead and drive off, no need to visit reception first. Okay? Straight to the car and out."

"It's not a car. It's a ute."

"Trust me, no-one will think you're doing a runner because I'm still here with Lulu, and check-out isn't until ten. You've got plenty of time."

My smile felt like a wobbling grimace. "I've never done this sort of thing before. Maybe you should do it. I'll stay here with the baby."

"Oh, come on, it's easy. All you need is a Phillip's head screwdriver. You've got one of those, haven't you?"

"Yes, in my tool kit in the ute."

"So what's the big deal?" Grinning and frowning at once, Rita shook her head as if goggling at my stupidity. "Relax, the licence plates on most cars are attached with a couple of teeny-weeny screws, nothing else. It'll take you no more than a minute. Whatever you do, though, don't come back with any personalised plates, for God's sake. Stick to the regular kind. And ignore any car that has its plates inside those little framed windows, okay?"

I nodded. Despite my shower and the steady, chilled breeze from the air conditioner, my swampy armpits stuck to my shirt and I could smell my own stink – or perhaps that was the funk of the motel room.

The baby twitched its limbs in jerky spasms as it drank the formula milk. It must have been hungry because it guzzled at the bottle, making contented *mmm* sounds after every swallow, and with every cell in my body, I wished that the baby was a million miles from here.

"Pick an older car," Rita continued, "but one that looks respectable. We don't want any plates off a crim's car."

I stood up. "Fine, I'll go to a supermarket or train station. There'll be plenty of cars to choose from there."

"No, Ronnie. Not unless you want to get filmed by CCTV cameras."

I hadn't thought of that. "You want me to find a quiet suburban street?"

"Aw, Christ, where are your brains? A nosy old biddy peeking through her venetian blinds will see you fucking about with a parked car, and be ringing the cops in two seconds flat. Do I have to think of everything?"

"I'm sorry."

"Get going. And try to use your noggin for once."

I paused at the door. "Should I throw my plates away?"

"Not yet. Keep them for now. Later, we'll chuck them where the cops won't ever find them, in a dam or a river someplace."

Spooked, I recalled the bridge near my house, where, last night, she'd made me pull over and stop the ute to let her toss something from her handbag into the murk of the creek below. What could the item have been? And why had its disposal meant more to her than a fast getaway?

"Hurry up, Ronnie," she said, clicking her fingers at me, snap snap snap. "We've got to get a move on. And don't forget breakfast on your way back. If you can't get plain croissants, get me a coffee scroll."

I let myself out. Apart from my ute, the car park held a yellow station wagon and a battered four-cylinder heap with rust eating at its doors. The sky was clear and blue, the air already warm. I started the ute, and got a fanfare of rock music; last night, Rita had changed the radio station. I reset it to my favourite, the one that plays the golden oldies, then drove out onto the ribbon of road.

There wasn't much traffic and only a few pedestrians at this early hour. Dingy shop fronts sagged shoulder to shoulder, looking tired and defeated – beaten down, broken, I thought miserably, just like me.

Despite Rita's instructions, I had no idea how to 'case' a suitable car for its licence plates. I drove in circles without purpose or direction. After about ten minutes, I pulled into a residential side street clotted with rundown weatherboards and fibro cement houses, and parked. Now what? I didn't know that either.

I went to switch off the ignition. Instead, my fingers hesitated over the key ring, over the tag that listed my name and address, over each key in turn – front door, back door, shed – and a mixture of longing and regret wrenched so hard at me, so viscerally, that it felt like my ribs would crack.

If I were at home, I reminisced, I'd be showered and shaved by now, whistling, frying up a plate of bacon and eggs while a pot of coffee perked on the stove. Being Tuesday, I'd be heading off first to mow lawns at the Sonnenschein place – Mrs Sonnenschein always giving me, without fail, a pint glass of raspberry cordial and a home-made brownie along with my cheque. Comforting memories, perhaps, but only for a moment; it soon occurred to me that I wouldn't stand in my kitchen ever again, and wouldn't work ever again for the Sonnenscheins, or any other of my clients. I had no choice but to continue with Rita's plan. Returning to my abandoned life, after what I had done, was impossible. Wasn't it?

An idea curled into my mind, softly, quietly. It took me a while to notice it.

I had another option, not yet considered: drive to the local police station and spill my guts to the first officer who'd listen to me.

I opened my eyes and sat up. Across the road in the gutter, a couple of sparrows fought over a crunch of food wrappers, chirping angrily. I gaped at them while the shocking idea firmed up a little more.

Well? Why not turn myself in and confess?

Our dream wasn't possible. No matter how much love and affection we gave it, no matter how hard we tried to be its parents, the baby wouldn't feel like ours; rather, it would be a constant, wearing reminder of our crime. Worse, Rita and I would be on the run forever – or, at least, until the police caught up with us – slumming on cash jobs, skulking from one anonymous bedsit or motel to another, always changing our names, never knowing if we were being watched, never able to let our guard down. And as for poor Mrs Whitmore... I groaned, wiping a trembling hand over my eyes. Worst of all, how could our life with the baby ever bring joy or contentment, knowing that poor Mrs Whitmore had to endure, every moment, year after year, an endless horror of grief and torment because of us, because of me, because of what I had done? Unthinkable.

If I went to the police, I began to figure, I had a chance to put everything right. I'd lead them to the motel, wait in the car park while the officers burst in with their guns drawn; Rita would *have* to surrender. Then I could deliver Abby Rose into Mrs Whitmore's arms, and after that, after finally doing *The Right Thing*, have my old life back.

Following, I supposed upon further reflection, some jail time.

What cheer I'd managed to drum up fizzled away. The thought of going to jail turned my bowels to ice. And what would I have upon my release? Nothing. My old life would be gone for good anyway. Mr and Mrs Whitmore would hate the very sight of me. So would the rest of my neighbours, and every one of my clients. The pensioners at the retirement village would spit in my face, including dear Mrs Caldecott, who had always treated me like a distant nephew of sorts. Oh, I'd have to move, I realised, have to start over somewhere else, but this time without Rita, this time as a hated ex-convict without the prospect of ever again finding another person on earth who would love me; the loneliness worse than before, much worse, since I would have the experience of Rita's love to mourn and miss and remember every day of my wretched life. Unthinkable.

By now, the sparrows in the gutter across the road had stopped fighting, the victor decided by secret bird signals. Unmolested, one of them pecked happily at a food wrapper, while the other watched from a distance. In my feverish state of mind, this little drama struck me as an omen, a critical sign from the gods, and I tried to figure out what it could possibly mean.

The radio station DJ piped up to announce the hour. In her young, breezy voice, the female newsreader told me that it was seven o'clock and already nineteen degrees in the city. Then she gutted me.

She said, "In the eastern suburbs last night, a twenty-eight-year-old woman was murdered and her newborn baby kidnapped in a brutal home invasion. Homicide detectives describe the crime scene as one of the worst they've seen."

It hit me in a nauseating, dislocating rush of physical sensations. The world dropped out from under and swung away, disappearing into a crazy, distant spiral, a dot on the event horizon.

Murdered?

On the radio came a male policeman, his voice crackling, tinny, recorded over a telephone line. He said, "It's a particularly heinous crime. We've had no word at this stage on the infant's welfare. Obviously, we're very concerned for her safety. We appeal to members of the public and ask that anyone with information which might help us with our investigation come forward."

That would be *me*.

The newsreader twice gave out the phone number to call Crime Stoppers. Immediately after, she offered an update on the road toll (three more deaths than at the same time last year, apparently, with cyclists and pedestrians over-represented in the statistics), talked about retailers experiencing their lowest Christmas sales since the last recession, and finished up her report with sporting scores. Next, a song came on, a peppy tune from the 80s, featuring multi-tracked harmonies and synthesisers.

12

I tried to kid myself. How about that for an atrocious crime, I thought, sighing and pondering sadly the decaying morals of Western society. And what a freakish coincidence that someone else's newborn had been kidnapped on the very same night we took Abby. Then my forehead hit the steering wheel.

When I came to, I was staring into the footwell's detritus: grit, twigs, dried-up gum leaves; my own crusted, muddy footprints. I twisted the car keys, killing the song on the radio, killing the ignition. Quietness settled inside the cab. Tyres swooshed softly on bitumen as the odd vehicle drove past on the main road nearby. Blood thundered in my ears.

I didn't know what to think; I gave up trying and watched the sparrows instead. The winner lost interest in the food wrappers and flew off. The loser hopped over and inspected the wrappers with a sideways tilt of the head, but didn't peck at them. I wondered if this scenario was some kind of omen too, but couldn't decide.

Time passed. Gradually, painfully, the truth began to gibber at me:

So that's how Rita had managed to take the baby from Mrs Whitmore...

Why I hadn't heard Mrs Whitmore screaming...

Why Rita had refused to put back the baby...
And didn't answer any of my questions.

Mrs Whitmore's fresh, plain and scrubbed face came to mind, and then her habitual ponytail worn long to her waist, her raucous hee-haw laugh, the way she would sing – in a pleasantly high, melodious register – every time she took in her washing from the Hills Hoist. Dizzy, I closed my eyes.

Murdered.

And yet... Rita had been so calm last night. If she'd really killed Mrs Whitmore, I argued with myself, then surely Rita would have appeared... upset? Agitated? Depressed? I didn't know. How does a killer act in the hours after taking a life?

I dragged open my heavy eyelids. Across the road, the second sparrow had gone; I felt oddly bereft. The food wrappers in the gutter stirred in the light breeze and I stared at them, confounded, with no idea what to do next. My mind felt sandblasted.

Clearly, I needed a long walk.

After locking the ute, I started back to the motel on foot, my legs boneless as if wading through water. The pavement along the main road was uneven, smashed. A bench at a tram-stop had missing slats with graffiti carved into it. Nearby, strapped to a telephone pole, an overflowing bin was buzzing with flies. What a god-awful neighbourhood, I thought, and felt like crying again.

A metallic screeching noise flung me against a low brick fence. The approaching tram eased off its brakes and chugged along its rails. A purple-haired girl sitting in the back glared at me with contempt while I clung to the fence in a half-crouch, a frightened animal. I wondered who she was and where she was going and whether later, if my part in the murder-kidnapping was ever discovered and reported on the television news, this sneering purple-haired girl would gasp, turn to whoever was sitting next to her on the couch and stammer, *Oh shit, I saw that man on the street and mistook him for a deranged idiot.*

The idea of it made me laugh out loud. The purple-haired girl – who had, I could now discern as the tram went by, a bunch of stud and hoop earrings crowded along her eyebrows and nose – turned in her seat to keep staring at me through the tram window, and I waved gaily, wildly, at her. She stuck up her middle finger. I laughed some more. After that, for about a minute, I waited on the footpath with my hands on my knees, trying to control my breathing, struggling to keep my thoughts in some kind of order.

Murdered.

Unbidden, I imagined slamming open the door to our motel room:

Rita jumps to her feet, too late, nowhere to run, there's one exit and I'm blocking it. This is for Mrs Whitmore, I say through gritted teeth. My hands close around Rita's throat, thumbs crossing over her windpipe, pressing, squeezing, crushing, her eyes goggling wide, as big as barnyard eggs, while the colour in her face changes from red to purple to black as I throttle, and keep throttling, until something grinds and snaps, daintily, like the delicate break of a chicken wishbone.

The fantasy was intoxicating enough to almost choke me.

Plodding one foot in front of the other, I made it past side streets and laneways to the outskirts of the shopping precinct. My shimmering image floated next to me in store windows as I passed a smattering of early-morning pedestrians. It wasn't long before the motel's yellow sign shone in the distance. I kept my eyes on it. And then, unexpectedly, I was outside the department store where, last night, I had encountered Santa Claus.

I stopped. Headless, ghost-white dummies in the display window flaunted bathers, summer dresses, crop tops, hipster jeans. Desiccated blowflies peppered the carpet, worn down to the webbing from years of relentless sunshine. The tableau struck me as allegorical, significant; I don't know why, except to suggest that people under pressure sometimes turn to superstition. My mother certainly did. Whenever Jesus Christ and the Bible failed her, which was often, she would hunt for signs and portents from the Spirit World for guidance; forever searching for the meaning behind coincidence and serendipity, always turning to me and remarking, finger wagging, *You see, pet? Do you see how the Conscious Universe talks to your mum?*

I had always looked back on Mum's neediness and her desperation for reassurance with some contempt. Until now.

Shielding my eyes with cupped hands against the glare, I put my face against the department store window. Everything was cut-price and cut-rate, tawdry, pitiable.

The motel sign beckoned. I pushed off from the store window and kept walking, swiping at tears with the back of my hands. As I crossed a street against the red light, a Volkswagen sedan that had right of way braked hard and skidded, sounding the horn, missing me by inches. I didn't care. I was already on the other side, tramping the footpath, aimed squarely at the iron gates of the motel entrance, hands jammed into my pockets, fingers clenched and aching.

13

Cool, dry air hit me from the wall-mounted air conditioner. Rita was sitting in the wing chair, crooning softly at the baby cradled in her lap. The baby, yawning, roamed its cross-eyed gaze about the motel room. It wore a purple and pink dress, more evidence of Rita's deceitful nature: she must have secretly bought that outfit herself, because I certainly didn't get anything like it at the supermarket.

Heart convulsing in my throat, I closed the motel door and engaged the bolt.

Without glancing up, Rita said, "Did you find licence plates okay?"

"We need to talk about something else first."

"Aw, look, isn't she beautiful? Just about the most beautiful thing I've ever seen. Aren't you, darling Lulu? Aren't you? Yes, you are."

With her head tipped forward like that and her hair swept off her shoulders, I could see the pulse throbbing in Rita's neck.

"You've got to tell me the truth," I said. "The truth about what you did."

She sighed and lifted the baby higher in her arms, nuzzling her cheek against its fuzzy wisps of blonde hair.

"Rita?" I said.

"Okay, fine, I'll tell you. Make me a coffee first."

I filled the kettle from the bathroom tap, plugged in the cord and flicked the switch – nice and steady, one thing at a time. I sat on one of the single beds to wait. When the kettle boiled, I poured out an instant coffee and placed it on the bedside table nearest to her. While I did these things, Rita watched me, silently and carefully.

Finally, she said, "So you've heard."

"On the radio, yes."

She nodded.

"Why did you do it?" I said. "Why?"

She gave a dismissive gesture. "Oh, for fuck's sake, how did you think I was going to take Lulu? Walk up and say please?" She kissed the baby's forehead. "And you're so beautiful, aren't you, Lulu? I'd do anything for you, wouldn't I, honey? Absolutely anything."

She put the baby on the other single bed, took up her coffee and, sipping at it, resumed her place in the wing chair with one leg delicately folded beneath her.

"You're a murderer," I whispered.

To my bewilderment, horror, fury, she actually smiled.

"And you're my accomplice," she said. "You look pretty pissed off. I suppose you're mad enough to kill me."

"Yes, I'd very much like to kill you." I interlaced my fingers together and squeezed to stop them from trembling. The ceiling hung low and the walls tightened around me. "How did you do it?"

"Fast."

"Tell me exactly how you killed Mrs Whitmore."

"It's better if I spare you the gory details."

"No, Rita. For once, I want you to be honest."

"Honest?" Her lips pulled into a sneer. "You really want to know? It'll stick in your head for a long time. You'll be dreaming about it years from now; an old codger with a walking frame and bad dreams every night."

"Tell me."

"Okay. Feel free to butt in if I'm not being juicy enough for you."

And this is what she said:

I ring the bell. It takes forever before she opens the door; I've got to ring another couple of times. She's wearing an ankle-length blue satin nightie and matching dressing gown, and open-toed scuffs like the kind you sometimes get for free in flash hotels. For a second, she's surprised to see me, giving me a blank face like she can't remember who I am. I stick out my hand and smile.

"Hello, Jennifer," I say. "Penelope Teasdale? District infant health-care nurse?"

She smiles back. "Oh yes, from the hospital. Please come in."

We go to the lounge room and it screams money: done out in glass and chrome and leather, every appliance top of the line, TV the size of a bus, a heap of fancy-arse paintings in big silver frames that would have cost a packet hanging on the walls. We're talking serious money. Through an archway is the kitchen. It's weird to see it from this angle for once, instead of through the hole in the fence. I've entered a kind of dream world.

"Can I get you something to drink?" she says to me. "Coffee? Fruit juice?"

Time is ticking, so I shake my head and say, "Let's get started, shall we? Perhaps you could take me to the baby."

She heads down the hall. My heels sink into the carpet pile. I tell you, this couple has cash to splash. I keep up the spiel the whole time. "Is your husband at home?" I say.

"Sorry, he just popped out to the supermarket."

"Oh, that's a pity. I wanted to talk to him about the different ways he can offer support. Is he helpful around the home?"

"Yes, very," she says, and rabbits on about how he cleans

the dunny, but I can't hear her any more. We're in the master bedroom. There's the bassinet.

And there's my Lulu.

And, oh Ronnie, she's just… so… *beautiful*, that it cuts me up inside. I think, well, I missed your first few days in the world, Lulu, but at least these people took fine care of you on my behalf.

"Do you need to check her?" she says.

As much as I want to hold my little girl, I have to get the business done first.

"I'll have a look at her in a minute," I say. "It's you I'm most concerned about. You had an episiotomy, is that right?"

That's a scalpel cut, Ronnie. To make the hole wider so the baby's head can come out. You see, I always do my homework. Nothing's left to chance.

"Yes," she says, "but I ripped right through it. Second-degree tear, apparently. The anti-inflammatory pills they gave me at the hospital aren't working. The stitches hurt like hell."

I make some oh-too-bad clucking noises. "It'll take a few weeks, I'm afraid," I say. "Now I'd like to see how you're healing up. Please lie down."

The doona is folded back to the foot of the bed, and the top sheet is kicked into a mess, like I'd disturbed her having a nap. She takes a seat, turns her back, lies down and starts hiking up her nightie. She's obviously done this for medical staff a few times because she knows the drill. While she's busy arranging herself and untwisting her clothes, I pull on my latex gloves.

"I'll check for obvious signs of infection first," I say.

"Okay," she says.

I reach in my handbag and grab the hammer, low on the shaft. I creep to the bed. She's on her side with one leg doubled up, the other lying straight, and her nightie bunched around her waist. Yuck; the sight of what's between her legs makes me want to spew. It's a blue and purple football down there, honest to God, all swollen up and with these nasty black stitches running over it. Lady, I think, if that's what childbirth does to a woman, better you than me.

I pick a spot on the skull, the flat bit above the ear. Lulu is gurgling behind me and moving about in her bassinet, like she's anxious to see me too.

"Not long now," I say to Lulu.

"That's fine, I don't mind," Jennifer Whitmore says, assuming I'm talking to her, and that makes me smile.

I whip the nightie and dressing gown up and over her head and in the next split-second, slam that hammer down hard –

WHAM

– like I'm trying to drive it straight through the bed.

Her body gives a heaving jerk. I hit her again. She starts yowling, and her legs jolt and kick like she's throwing a fit, and I'm hitting and hitting and hitting, and having to kneel on her and lean on her because she's fighting to get up.

The nightie over her head gets soaked real quick. I have to haul up the doona to contain the splatter, meanwhile keep hitting her through it, and keep a knee on her back at the same time. I hit and I hit and soon she's not moving. The doona has a spot of red about the size of a twenty-cent piece. I aim at it. The red spot gets bigger. I keep hitting until it sounds like I'm pounding into porridge and I stop. All of that takes about a minute.

I take a breather. You know, she has a swanky collection of clothes in her walk-in robe. Her shoes are size nine, though, too big for me. Once I've got my breath, I put the hammer back inside the plastic bag in my handbag, take off the gloves and stash them too. I pick up Lulu, kiss her on her sweet little mouth, and race down the hallway, open the back door, go to the fence.

Call out to you, Ronnie.

Wait for you to help me.

14

You see?" Rita said from the bathroom doorway. "I warned you, didn't I?"

My stomach, well and truly empty, kept retching anyway. After the spasms finally eased, I let go of the toilet bowl and hauled myself to my feet, leaning against the cistern until my head stopped spinning. When I felt steady enough, I flushed the toilet.

"Leave me alone," I said, turning on the basin taps, grabbing the soap. "Let me clean up in peace."

As I rinsed my mouth and began washing my hands, Rita leaned against the doorway, and said, "You're such a soft cock, Ronnie."

"Go away."

"Make me. Hah, that's something I'd like to see. What were you saying before about wanting to kill me?"

I put the bar of soap in the dish and flexed my hands. They felt strong enough to possibly strangle a kitten, if I tried hard enough. She was right to mock me. I deserved it, and more.

She continued, "You didn't come back with breakfast, so I suppose you didn't get any licence plates either."

Drying my face and hands on a towel, I didn't bother to reply.

"So where's the car?" she said. "It's not out front."

"It's a ute. And I parked it a few blocks from here."

"Huh? What for? Jesus, you want to get to Queensland or not? Stop piss-farting around; go get the fucken car and a set of plates right now. And don't forget breakfast this time, I'm starving."

She headed out to the main room, flopped across the empty bed and switched on the television with the remote control. Her thumb jabbed repeatedly at the channel selector.

"Oh, wow," she said, her face brightening, "we've got cable."

She settled on a channel. Two presenters of an early morning breakfast program yabbered and giggled at each other. I stood at the foot of the bed and stared at Rita until, sighing, she muted the television.

"What?" she said.

"If I go," I said carefully, measuring every word, "what's stopping me from walking straight to the nearest police station and turning you in?"

Her eyes narrowed. "A little thing called self-preservation."

"Maybe I'm ready to go to jail and pay for what I've done."

"Yeah? A murder conviction carries a pretty long sentence."

"That's true, but they'll be arresting you for the murder, not me. I'll tell the police exactly what happened."

She mulled this over, and sat up. "No, that's not how it'd play. Let's pretend for a minute that you've got the balls to dob. If the coppers busted in here, I'd collapse into tears and cling to them in relief because I'm your hostage, you get it? You beat me, raped me, forced me to help you. If I didn't, you threatened to kill me just like you killed Jennifer Whitmore."

My mind whirled around, tried to find something to cling to, found very little. In he-said-she-said cases, the woman usually wins the sympathy of the police and the courts; at least, that's how it works in the movies.

"By the time I get through telling my side of the story," Rita went on, "everyone in the world is going to hate your guts. People will want to stick the knife into you, coppers included. You'll be bashed resisting arrest. You'll be bashed in remand. They'll need police protection to get you to court in one piece. And how do you think the prison inmates are going to treat you? Every scumbag in there will want to be the hero that shanks the mummy-killer."

I groped for the wing chair and sat down. Rita laughed, slipped off the bed and came over to me, putting her arms around me and kissing the top of my head.

"Don't shit your pants, dummy," she said. "This is all just talk."

"Oh? It sounds like you're threatening me."

Taking the lapels of my shirt collar in both of her little hands, her expression serious, eyes flat and cold, she said, "I'm not threatening you. I'm reminding you." With a pat on my cheek and a quick smile, she resumed her seat on the bed.

As she reached for the television remote, I said, "There's physical evidence that you killed her and I didn't. What about the hammer?"

"It's at the bottom of a creek. Remember when we drove from your place last night, I got you to park on that bridge?"

I nodded. "You know I could direct police divers to the exact spot."

"Yeah, but I wore latex gloves. If coppers find the hammer, the only fingerprints on it will be yours. Whose hammer do you think I used?"

Prickles crawled over my scalp. The noose that Rita had placed about my neck, deliberately or otherwise, was becoming clearer by the second. I tried to keep my face as expressionless as she was so effortlessly keeping hers.

"Aw, don't worry about it any more," she continued. "None of this is ever going to happen. You'd never give me up to the coppers. You love me, right? Besides, if I thought you were planning to turn me in, I'd skip."

"Run away? No point; I could still tell the police who you are."

She grinned. "And who am I, exactly?"

Who indeed? Obviously, I had no idea. "I can tell them where you lived."

"At the Foster dump? Ellen Kennedy lived there, not me."

"What about the people at the retirement village? Your customers know you."

"They know me as Rita McNaughton."

"Isn't that your real name?"

She got up, came over and perched on my knee, putting both arms around me. "Listen, Ronnie, we're sticking to our plan. By sundown tomorrow, we'll be a family starting its new life in Queensland. Isn't that what you want: you, me and Lulu? Isn't that what you've always wanted?"

I hesitated and searched her face, looking for clues, wondering if this was some kind of trap or another lie. I couldn't read her. Rita's face looked tender and sincere. I wondered if I'd ever been able to read her.

She leaned down and kissed me, slowly and deeply. When she at last pulled away, she whispered, "I love you. Okay?"

I know what I should have done: pushed her away and called the police. Instead I hugged her tight.

She kissed me again, this time on the cheek, and said, "Good boy. Now go get your car and some plates."

15

I headed outside, closing the door of the motel room quietly behind me so as not to wake the baby. I started walking, squinting in the glare, the deep blue of the sky auguring a beautiful summer's day.

Murdered.

It didn't seem possible. None of it did. I dragged the mobile phone from my pocket and switched it on. There were nineteen messages, some eighteen or nineteen more than usual. I didn't bother to check them. Instead, I scrolled through my address book and dialled.

Mr Dabrowski answered after the fifth ring. "Hello?"

As if I'd expected my call to reach an answering machine, the familiar sound of his voice surprised me; next, it tamped my throat. Seconds passed before I could stutter out the words, "Good morning, Mr Dabrowski. This is Ronald Spooner, your neighbour from across the road. Sorry to be calling so early, I hope I didn't get you out of bed."

Dead air. Electrified, stupefied dead air.

A disquieting prescience made the sweat break out across my face. I wanted to hang up. Instead, I said, "Can you hear me, sir?"

A noisy exhalation, then: "Holy mother of God. Are you *shitting* me? Is this some kind of joke? Because I'm not laughing."

"No, Mr Dabrowski, it's me. It's Ron." More blowing, more gasping, as if he'd been running laps around an oval. It crossed my mind that he may have been having a heart attack right there on the phone. "Mr Dabrowski, are you all right?"

"You're in a whole heap of trouble, mate," he said. "The police are after you."

My mouth dried up. I stopped walking and propped against a fence. "Me?" I said at last. "What would they want with me?"

"Don't act cute. I know what you did, I saw you, for the love of Christ; I fixed the goddamned baby capsule for you. Come on back and clear this thing up."

So it was true. What I'd heard on the news report, everything in Rita's story. And as I'd feared, Mr Dabrowski had told his suspicions to the police.

In a rush, panicking now, I said, "It wasn't my fault. She made me do it."

"Who? Jenny Whitmore? That poor beautiful young girl?" His puffing hitched, and he made odd strangling noises. "God almighty, Ron, it's beyond belief. What could have made you do such a thing?"

"No, not me: Rita. Rita McNaughton did it."

"Who in blazes is Rita?"

"The woman I was with last night, remember? The woman in the passenger seat of the ute."

"I didn't see anyone else in the ute, Ron, no-one but you."

A headache mushroomed from the tightening muscles in my neck, a thrumming pain that spanned my skull from one temple to the other. "How is Mr Whitmore?" I said.

"As you'd expect: in a million pieces, doped up to the eyeballs. He's at his mum's. Oh, holy mother of God," Mr Dabrowski said, breaking in on himself as if remembering who he was talking to, what he was talking about. "Why did you call?"

That stumped me. "I don't know. I suppose I should say goodbye."

"Wait a minute, Ron. The little one. Alive or dead?"

"The baby's fine."

Frantic garbled sounds and hiccupping breaths suggested that Mr Dabrowski was crying. My finger hovered over the phone ready to cut the call.

His wife's concerned voice sounded in the background, but clear and close, like she was standing right in front of him. I imagined her with both hands held flat against his chest, a beseeching look on her bloated face.

"Henry," she said, "for goodness sake, what's happened, who is it?"

He must have put the receiver against his palm because the voices became muffled. "Ron Spooner, of all people," he said. "Mavis, it's Ron from across the road."

"Hang up," she shrieked. "Hang up on him."

They argued and tussled with the phone until Mr Dabrowski came on the line, puffing. "Ron, listen to me. Give yourself up. Call the police and tell them where you are."

A debilitating weariness closed my eyes.

When I didn't answer, Mr Dabrowski pressed on, asking, "Are you still in the country?"

"I'm still in Melbourne."

"Where? At someone's house? Do you know the address?"

"I don't know where I am, exactly. We booked into a motel. Mr Dabrowski, would you do me a small favour?"

"Depends on what it is."

"I left my back door open last night. I'd be grateful if you'd go over and secure it for me. Just unsnib the deadlock and shut the door, that's all you need to do."

"Sorry. Even if I wanted to, Ron, I couldn't get near the place for the coppers."

Coppers? Drawing a sharp breath, I said, "Have any of them gone inside?"

"Yeah, by the truckload."

What? I could hardly believe it. Police officers were *in my house*? Opening drawers, pawing through belongings? Blood flushed my cheeks, a combination of outrage and agonised embarrassment. What if they found my collection of men's magazines and DVDs? My attempts at poetry? And dear God, my diaries? Oh, this was too awful to contemplate.

"Please," I said, desperate, close to tears, "you've got to go over there immediately and tell the police they have no cause to search my house. Rita McNaughton, the cleaning lady, killed Mrs Whitmore, not me. They should be searching Rita's place, not mine. Would you tell them that for me? Please, Mr Dabrowski. This is incredibly important."

"You helped this Rita woman get away with the baby? Is that it?"

"Yes, but –"

"Sweet Mary, mother of Jesus," he moaned, and started weeping in earnest.

The sound of his bellowing sobs released my own. I hung my head. Tears dripped steadily onto my shirt. In a strange way, it was comforting to be crying with Mr Dabrowski, the two of us together, lifelong neighbours sharing a common loss.

Shocking me from my mournful reverie, Mrs Dabrowski's voice shrilled into my ear, "You animal! You stinking scum! You'll burn in hell for what you did, you bastard. Satan will stick you with his pitchfork and the – "

In quick, panicky movements, as if the phone was a hot coal I couldn't bear to touch, I hung up, switched it off and pocketed it within a second.

Once my head cleared, I continued to plod one foot in front of the other. Soon, I reached the strip, now crisscrossed with early morning shoppers. How many days until Christmas? I couldn't remember. But I must have been the only person without any shopping bags. Perhaps that was my undoing, the factor that made me stand out.

16

Something hit my leg. A child of about seven years of age, a boy holding his mother's hand, had walked straight into me.

"Whoops," I said. "Are you all right?"

The child stared up, drilling a finger determinedly into one of his crusty nostrils. Ready to apologise, I turned my attention to the mother, an attractive stranger with dark hair and eyes, who was glaring at me, about to tell me off, until her face went blank and another expression took its place: one of fearful, wary recognition.

Recognition!

My heart stopped. Gasping, I hurried past her. My photograph must be plastered over the television news.

That ghastly thought turned my head into a neon balloon. *Look here*, my giant balloon-head beamed to everyone in the shopping precinct, *it's Ronald Brian Spooner, accused mummy-killer and baby-napper, walking amongst you; make a citizen's arrest, call the police, capture him any way you can.*

God, there were so many people.

I kept my head low and hid behind my hand, trying to act natural as if I was shading my eyes from the sun or suffering from a headache, which, incidentally, was true on both counts. Bodies occasionally knocked against me. Every touch made me flinch. Maybe it wasn't a shopper's elbow but a police officer's hand, with a cudgel or even a gun brandished in the other, an upholder of the law who would swing me around, hit me straight on the jaw, make me cower before the might of uniform and badge. I walked faster.

The shops behind me at last, I rushed by dozens of weatherboard or fibro houses, their front lawns as uniformly dry and brown as doormats. I'd parked my ute in a residential side street named, ironically, 'Haven'. When I was close enough to read its name on the signpost, I broke into a jog. Turning the corner, I pulled up short, my wobbling knees almost felling me.

My ute was gone.

I stumbled along the footpath, scanning the ground this way and that, as if my ute had somehow shrunk to toy-size. Opposite, lying in the gutter, were the food wrappers fought over by the two sparrows. This was definitely the right place. My ute *should* be there. I looked and looked and kept looking, trying to force the vehicle to materialise through willpower alone, but it was no use. My ute was gone.

Gone, gone, gone.

My. Ute. Was. Gone.

Stolen? Or maybe towed away? I searched for a 'no parking' sign and couldn't find one. There was another possibility, a dreadful one that I could barely stomach: a police car on regular patrol had spotted my ute and called in the licence plate number. No doubt, my ute was sitting in a forensic garage somewhere getting dismantled and dusted for prints... which could only mean that this particular street was presently under surveillance.

I flattened myself against a sagging wooden fence. When nothing happened, when the battalion of officers with shotguns and body armour failed to spring out in a circle around me, I started legging it back to the motel.

What would Rita say when I told her the ute was gone?

I considered stealing a car but dismissed that idea almost as soon as it came to me. My entire life has been a lawful one; I didn't know the first thing about breaking into a car and hot-wiring an engine. I've never stolen anything in my life.

Except for a baby. Except for that.

I trudged on, trying to imagine Rita's next move.

For argument's sake, I decided that she didn't have any feelings for me, and that she was waiting for me in the motel room for one reason and one reason only: transport. I didn't have transport. That made me… expendable.

How would she react?

Well, she might take off with the baby, leaving me behind. Or she'd dump both me and the baby at the motel and take off alone. That would be the smartest option. Without Rita, I'd be captured in an instant. The police wouldn't believe my story; I'd take the blame for the whole thing and go to jail. Rita could get away clean and try again with another woman's child at a later date. It sounded like a promising theory until I conceded that abandoning the baby was the last thing Rita would do. As far as she was concerned, the baby was hers; she'd move heaven and hell to keep it. Hadn't she already?

The most logical solution from Rita's perspective, I finally realised, and the only option that made sense, was for her to kill me.

My pumping legs slowed to an ambling pace. Taking one point at a time, I systematically tested my new theory for glitches. I couldn't find any.

According to Mr Dabrowski, the police weren't aware of Rita's involvement. Therefore, I was the only person who knew what she'd done, the only thing that linked her to the murder and kidnapping. If I were dead, the police investigation would grow as cold as my corpse; Rita would be free to live her life with the baby, and have no fear of ever being tied to her crimes. Perfect.

I started wondering how she'd do it. No doubt she had any number of weapons stashed amongst her belongings, including the pocket knife I'd found in her hessian bag. A carving knife in a self-sharpening holder, a screwdriver with its tip honed to a keen edge. Even one of those combs with a steel handle as thin as a knitting needle would do it. But when would she strike?

Unquestionably, she would never try to kill me at the motel. There were too many witnesses, too many surfaces with her fingerprints, and the approaching 10 a.m. checkout wouldn't give her enough time to escape. Instead, she'd probably come up with a scheme to lure me to an isolated place where my remains would stay hidden for a long, long time, if not forever. Oh yes, I mused, chuckling, tears filling my eyes, I'd end up buried in bushland somewhere, or dumped at an abandoned property, or left to dissolve at the bottom of a river if she managed to weigh me down with enough stones. A resourceful, calculating woman like Rita was capable of just about anything.

I kept trudging. The sunlight reflected in bright spangles off every surface and lanced into my eyes. The constant squinting helped along my headache until my scalp felt as tender as a boil. In despair, I thought fleetingly of going to the police, but I didn't have the guts. Shame made me wish I were dead. And for one crazed instant, I felt glad to be walking back to the hands of my executioner. I wanted to die, I deserved to die, and Rita would mete out the justice.

The tolling of a bell brought me to a standstill. I looked around. Up ahead, outside the department store, roamed Santa Claus. Faltering, I planned to cross the road to avoid him. With one foot in the gutter, however, it dawned on me in a warm, blossoming wave that my lifelong fear of Santa had been designed, meaningfully and purposefully, to bring this very moment to my attention. Quite obviously, I was supposed to communicate with him, and through him, with the Conscious Universe.

Clenching my teeth, sobbing and laughing, I made straight for Santa.

17

The shopping precinct thronged with pedestrians. I stood in a doorway and watched Santa. He had a battered brass pot on a tripod next to him and was handing out lollies to the children, sounding his bell every now and again.

"Ho, ho, my little angel," he said to one girl of about three years of age, who shrank against her mother. "Oh, you're not scared of dear old Santa, are you love?" he continued, and the girl mashed her face against her mother's hip. He added, "I've got your Chrissie presents in my sleigh back home. I'll be dropping them off in a few days, what do you think of that, hey?"

The girl wasn't having a bar of it. I knew exactly how she felt. The mother said a few words to Santa I couldn't catch; probably an explanation or an apology of some kind. Santa waved it away and pressed lollies into the mother's hand.

"No worries," he said. "Merry Christmas, anyway."

The girl, heading off with her mother, glanced back. Santa wiggled his fingers goodbye and she quickly looked away. He continued his performance, bellowing ho-ho-ho, and ringing his bell.

After a while, he noticed me standing there. He kept looking over. My presence must have irritated him because he finally put one fist on his hip and said to me, "If you want a lolly, come over and ask for one, why don't you?"

I shuffled forward, my heart flopping against my ribs. Santa was probably in his sixties, with a lined, pouched face that spoke of too much booze and too many cigarettes; his nose looking like it had been broken a couple of times and left to set by itself. *He's an ordinary man trying to make an honest living,* I reminded myself, *and I'm too old to be frightened.*

"Lolly?" he said.

They were the type I like, boiled ones in cellophane, but I shook my head.

"Okay, suit yourself. Have you been a good boy for Santa?"

I shook my head again.

"No? Aw, too bad. Don't expect me to drop through your chimney any time soon." He rang his bell. "Ho ho ho, merry Christmas everyone. Merry Christmas."

He attended to a couple of children, then turned back and appeared surprised to find me still there. I tried to smile.

"Shove off," he said without moving his lips, as he reached into his pot for another handful of lollies.

"Have you got a message for me?" I said.

He pulled a face. "Yeah, I have. Your Martian friends are landing tomorrow. Now piss off."

"I need to speak to you."

"What for? You want my job? Go see the assistant manager."

"I'm in trouble and I need help."

"And what do I look like to you, the bloody Salvos? Get going."

"Please. You saw me last night. I was in the ute."

He was handing out lollies to a knot of excited children who'd gathered around for the booty. I wasn't sure if he was listening to me; I pressed on anyway.

"I held up the traffic, remember? The tooting horns? You pointed at me. You pointed at me and rang your bell."

"Oh yeah, the sook," he said, amused, and grabbed some more lollies out of his brass pot. He shot an interested glance at me, waiting for me to go on.

"Yes, that's right, the sook," I said, encouraged. "This sounds ridiculous, but I don't know what to do. I'm hoping you could tell me."

Suspicious, he weighed me up with narrowed eyes. Then he grabbed the brass pot and tripod, and motioned with his head for me to follow him.

We went into a narrow laneway that ran alongside the department store. At the end of the store's brick wall was a flight of wooden stairs that led to a door on the second floor. Santa had a rest area set up under the stairs with a folding plastic chair, and nearby on a crate, a bottle of soft drink, a crumpled packet of smokes, and a newspaper. I stared at the newspaper in dread. To my relief, I saw when I got closer that it was folded at the racing section. On the front page, I had no doubt, must be a black and white photograph of my face.

Santa ducked under the stairs and sat on the chair. After taking off the fake beard, he pulled a cigarette from the packet and lit it with an old tin lighter. The crowd crisscrossed at the alley's mouth. I twisted my fingers into knots. He snapped the lighter shut, shoved it back in his pocket, took a slow, thoughtful drag on the cigarette and skewed an eye at me.

"What's your name?" he said.

I paused.

"Come on, it's not a tough one," he said.

"Ron."

"Pleased to meet you, Ron. I'm Max."

Another long drag showed off the deep creases around his mouth. He held the smoke in his lips while he struggled out of the red jacket. Underneath, he wore a tattered singlet. Faded blue tattoos ranged over his arms. One tattoo was a sailing boat, I think, the others a collection of blurred, shapeless blobs.

"You've got five minutes, Ron. That's my full smoko. What's on your mind?"

Tears threatened; I could feel my chin quivering. "I don't even know where to start," I said. "I'm sorry; I think I'm wasting your time."

"Here," he said, dragging out a milk crate from under the stairs and up-ending it. "Take a load off."

I sat down. The folded newspaper kept nagging at the corner of my eye, until I couldn't take the suspense any more.

"Max," I said, "don't you recognise me?"

"No. Should I?"

"My face is everywhere. Just before, a woman on the street knew who I was."

"And did you know her?"

I shook my head. "This is going to sound crazy but I'm out of options. My mother used to tell me that if you paid close enough attention, the universe gave you clues about what to do. I'm on the lookout for omens today. You seem to fit the bill."

"Oh yeah?" he said, smiling gently. "I thought omens were objects or birds."

"I'm not sure. I think an omen can be anything, even a person."

"All right, I won't argue with you on that. So I'm an omen. I've been called a lot of things, but that's a new one. What about the woman on the street you mentioned. Was she an omen too?"

"I don't know. I'm new at this, I can't tell."

Max blew a fat smoke ring and admired it for a moment, then broke it with a stab of his cigarette. "If you don't mind me asking, Ron, are you on any meds at the moment?"

"Meds?"

"Medications. Is a doctor treating you for anything?"

"No."

He regarded me steadily. "You remind me of my brother, Paulie. He used to pull stunts like this. Back then, there wasn't much you could do for schizos."

A slow flush heated my face. Max stamped the butt under his heel then reached into his cigarette packet. I noticed the tip of his thumb was missing.

"You know what I think?" he said, and paused to light the smoke. "I think you should go to a doctor and tell him about these omens you're after."

Groaning, I dropped my forehead into my hands. "Please, you've got to believe me, I'm not mentally ill. I'm not, I swear."

Max dragged on his smoke, looked at his watch.

"Okay, look," I continued, "a woman tricked me into doing a terrible thing and now I'm in a lot of trouble."

"The same woman who recognised you on the street?"

"No, a different one. And I suspect she's planning to kill me."

He nodded. "Are you on any drugs? Meth, LSD, that kind of thing?"

"No, of course not."

"Of course not, huh?" He sighed, and slapped my knee. "All right, you don't have to lay it out for me. You want my advice, so I'll give it to you."

The story he told, slick and practiced like a speech learned by rote, suggested he'd told it to anyone who stood still long enough to listen.

He said, "I used to be a drinker. I loved beer like you wouldn't believe, more than my wife, my kids, my job, my friends, everything. One night a few years ago, I went to my local and woke up four days later in a caravan park halfway across the country, with no recollection as to how I got there or what I'd been doing. It scared the shit out of me. So I cleaned up my act. You need to do the same."

He leaned in close; I could have counted the blood vessels in the yellowed whites of his eyes.

He added, "You want to lose the next twenty, thirty years of your life?"

Images of a prison yard flashed through my mind. "That's the last thing I want to do," I whispered.

"Then you have to kill your demon, Ron," he said. "If you want any kind of life, take my advice. Kill your demon."

18

Max ground his cigarette stub underfoot, stood, wiped his hand along the grimy leg of his pants and made to shake with me. I got up too, suddenly woozy, and took his hand. The palm was callused, as if used to hefting axes and shovels. I wondered if he'd done any jail time; it felt too late to ask.

"I'll be seeing you, Ron," he said.

He pulled on the Santa jacket and picked up the beard. Next, he reached behind his chair to a cardboard box containing lolly bags. He selected a bag, opened it, poured the lollies into his brass pot, and flung the empty bag towards the overstuffed dumpsters that lined the brick wall on the other side of the laneway. The bag fluttered to the ground, skipped in the breeze, and ended up at the foot of a cyclone wire fence, caught in a dead end with a heap of other rubbish. Could that be, I thought, another omen? Was I the plastic bag?

I turned to Max for clarification but he was already gone. After a couple of beats, I heard his bell ringing again. I swiped my hand across my face and flicked off the sweat.

Kill my demon.

My legs couldn't hold me up. I sat on the milk crate again, forced my mind into focus, and started hashing out a plan. Thanks to Santa's wisdom, one thing soon became perfectly self-evident: I had to kill Rita before she killed me.

And if I was smart about it, I slowly began to appreciate, I could get my life back, unscathed.

Somehow, with or without ready transport, I'd convince her to keep travelling with me. Later, in a secluded place, I'd kill her, dump the body. I would have to be careful. There couldn't be a trace of my DNA under her fingernails, for instance. And no blood; I couldn't afford one spot of her blood on me anywhere. The method needed some thought. If I choked her with my bare hands, for instance, forensic scientists would somehow figure out from the bruise pattern that I'd done it. A rope or chain, maybe... Once she was dead, I'd put the baby in a heavily-populated area like a shopping mall so it's discovered quickly and taken to the police. Then I'd report my ute missing. Go home.

The police would turn up, arrest me, take me to headquarters, and interrogate me; the interview taking place in a small windowless room, a video camera taping me as I'm sitting at the table with a timid, bewildered look, an innocent man inadvertently caught up in a crime; a detective seated across from me, his interrogation playing out something like this:

HIM: *Rita came to you with her baby niece, you say?*

ME: *Yes. I was to drive Rita and the baby to the baby's father in Ballarat. Rita's sister was in hospital for a day procedure and had to stay overnight because of complications.*

HIM: *So you bought a baby seat?*

ME: *Yes. My neighbour installed it for me, Mr Dabrowski.*

HIM: *You booked into a Melbourne motel that night with Rita and the baby. Why didn't you drive straight to Ballarat?*

ME: *Rita had a migraine, and wanted to wait 'til morning to make the trip.*

HIM: *Why didn't you turn around and drive home?*

ME: *Rita insisted we stay at a motel. It didn't make sense to me either. Look, am I in trouble? I don't know why I'm here.*

HIM: *We'll get to that in a minute. You booked into the motel under assumed names. Can you explain that?*

ME: *We did?*

HIM: *You sound surprised.*

ME: *I am. Gosh, that's news to me. I had no idea. Rita checked us in while I took care of the luggage. Why on earth would she use an assumed name?*

HIM: *To cover her tracks. The baby wasn't her niece. Brace yourself, Mr Spooner: Rita kidnapped the baby from strangers.*

ME: *Good Lord! Kidnapped? Are you sure?*

HIM: *Very sure. You haven't seen the news? Read any papers?*

ME: *I've been too busy looking after the baby. Kidnapped? Oh my God.*

HIM: *What happened to your ute?*

ME: *Someone stole it. Rita left the motel and came back with a car I've never seen before, and took off with the baby, leaving me behind.*

HIM: *We found the baby this morning abandoned in a shopping centre. She's back safe and sound with her father.*

ME: *What a relief. And Rita?*

HIM: *We're still looking.*

ME: *I hope you find her. She said something about moving to Queensland; perhaps you could start searching for her there. Gosh, I can't understand how she got me mixed up in her evil plot. I feel like such a dunce.*

HIM: *Oh, please don't be hard on yourself, Mr Spooner. It sounds like this Rita woman is a nasty piece of work. She had everybody fooled.*

ME: *If I can help you in any way, please let me know.*

HIM: *Of course. Now if you'll excuse me, I'm off to make a press statement to exonerate you from any part in this crime.*

ME: *What? You thought I was involved?*

HIM: *It looked that way for a while but now we know we made a mistake. Please accept my sincere apologies. You're walking out of here a free man. You can go back to your life exactly as it was before. No hard feelings, Mr Spooner?*

ME: *No hard feelings, Detective.*

This fantasy produced a sense of calm that relaxed me like a hot bath at the end of a long day. I opened my eyes and surveyed Max's cigarette butts mashed into the footpath, the rubbish flattened by the breeze against the cyclone fence, and the dumpsters. I felt a lifting of spirits. My plan was possible. I just had to keep my nerve.

I hurried out of the alley. Max, once again ho-ho-ho-ing and ringing his bell outside the department store, had his back to me; he wouldn't see my waved farewell. Was that a good omen or a bad one? Hard to tell – I decided that it was good.

19

Jogging back to the motel, I puzzled over the major sticking point of my plan: the missing ute. How could we get to Queensland without it? Rita would no doubt veto the idea of public transport. I wasn't keen on taking a bus or train either, as a matter of fact, out of fear of getting recognised again. Maybe we could ring a taxi company and ask them to send a cab that's fitted with a baby capsule – unless cabs don't come with baby capsules. But what else could we do? Hitchhike? Forget it; not with a baby. For a while, I felt helpless. How should I broach the subject of transport? I didn't know. As I slipped the key into our room door, I hoped that an answer would occur to me on the fly.

"I'm back," I said, simultaneously remembering that I'd failed – again – to purchase any breakfast. No doubt Rita would be angry about that too.

But I was invisible – Rita had eyes only for the baby. Whispering the loving babble that mothers have been crooning to their infants since the world began, Rita was lying on one of the single beds, curled on her side with the baby asleep in the crook of one arm. What a beautiful sight. For a moment, the tempting mirage of our life in Queensland shimmered in my mind's eye.

Brushing that away, I picked up the motel phone and ordered from reception two full breakfasts to be brought to our room. There, I thought, problem solved. My decisiveness, my taking control of the breakfast situation, helped to put steel in my spine;

before this whole sordid, miserable saga came to its bloody end, I wanted answers.

When I hung up, I took a seat on the other single bed and said, "Why can't you have children of your own?"

Rita's gaze flicked at me for a moment before settling back on the baby's profile. She began singing a soft lullaby.

"What's wrong with you down there?" I continued. "You must tell me."

The lullaby stopped. "No," she said. "I'm not talking about it."

"You have to. Don't you see? If we're to be man and wife, if we're to be good parents, we have to trust each other. Now tell me what made you sterile." When she didn't answer, I said, "As your fiancé, I have a right to know."

Her gaze crept from the baby's face to mine. Finally, she muttered, "Scars."

"Scars? What kind of scars?"

"Ones on the inside."

"From what?"

"Injuries."

"What kind of injuries?"

Eventually, she said, "The kind that little girls sometimes get if their mums aren't fussy about the boyfriends they bring home."

"What do you mean? Did one of your mother's boyfriends beat you?"

"Oh Jeez, Ronnie," she said, struggling to sit up without disturbing the baby. "I'm not spelling it out."

The baby kicked its feet, and dropped back to sleep. Rita went over to the bench, switched on the kettle, and started fussing with sachets of sugar and instant coffee, her back square to me, her shoulders set. Understanding slowly dawned. Oh, poor Rita; my poor, darling Rita.

"Didn't your mum know?" I said.

"Yeah, she knew."

Just didn't care. I went over and put my arms around her. Time heals all wounds, so they say, but it's not true: only love can do that. Love would rinse away her bad memories and reveal the original Rita that lay hidden beneath, the Rita that she was meant to be from the beginning, before life twisted her out of shape.

"How did you cope?" I said.

She leaned back against me, saying in a flat tone, "I ran away."

"Where did you go?"

"Anywhere. Everywhere. Nowhere."

I tightened my arms about her. During my initial visit to her bedsit, Rita had told me that, as a child, she'd wanted to be a ballerina. Alone on the streets, that innocent dream of hers must have felt impossibly far away.

"Did you ever go back home?" I said.

"No."

"Keep in contact with any relatives? A niece, perhaps?"

"No."

"And you've never given birth."

"What are you getting at, Ronnie?"

"It must be you in the photograph."

She stiffened and pulled away. "You looked in my purse?"

"When you're so secretive, Rita, you don't give me any choice."

The kettle, its water bubbling frantically, switched off. She put out her hand but I got there first, picking up the kettle and pouring the coffees myself in case she had a mad urge to fling boiling water at me.

Cautiously, I held out her cup. Instead of throwing it, she took the cup to the wing chair and sat down. I resumed my seat on the single bed.

"I've got one more question," I said.

She pinched at the bridge of her nose. "Do you really need to know all the ins and outs of a cat's arse?"

"When it comes to my wife-to-be, then yes; yes I do."

She looked up at me with a crooked grin. For the first time, I perceived the weariness in her face, her pallor, the skin under her eyes ringed with circles as dark as bruises. What a strain this dreadful situation must be for her too, I realised with a start. Here I am assuming that I'm the only one under threat of a nervous breakdown, but look at her... *just look at her.*

Gently, I said, "Rita McNaughton isn't your name."

At last, she shook her head.

"What is it?"

"I knew you'd forget. We decided on Melanie Andrews, remember? And you're Frank. That's what I wrote in the motel register last night."

"Stop it, Rita."

She looked away and sipped at her coffee.

"The name your mother gave you," I said. "No more games."

"All right." Her shoulder gave a noncommittal twitch. "Louise."

"Louise?" The air in the room thinned out. "The same name you gave to the Whitmore baby?"

"Don't make a big deal out of it."

"Oh, good Lord, you gave the baby your own name?"

"This is why I can't tell you anything."

"So who called you Lulu?"

"Nobody."

"Who? Tell me."

"All right: my grandmother."

I stared at Rita. She stared back at me with an uncertain, defiant smile.

This insane caper of hers began to make sense. I'm no psychologist, but even I could see the design: through the

Whitmore baby, Rita hoped to give herself a second chance at childhood, this time as the loving mother who would make sure that Louise-version-two grew up safe, protected, happy; a little girl who could, if she wanted, confidently dream of becoming a ballerina one day, and take as many dancing lessons as she desired.

Oh God.

A scalding rush of bile flooded my throat. I scrambled to the bathroom and closed the door. As I vomited, again, into the toilet, I heard the television start up, the audio jumping staccato as Rita flipped from one channel to the next. Within seconds, the baby started crying. The sound from the television stopped. Rita spoke to the baby in low, murmuring tones. My eyes shut, I spat repeatedly into the bowl, the rising stink causing my stomach to churn again.

Rita shrieked in a panicky, yelping pitch, "Aw, *fuck* no."

20

Hurriedly, I flushed the toilet and flung open the bathroom door. Rita was kneeling on the carpet in front of the muted television, not two feet away from the flickering screen, white-faced, with the squalling baby clutched at her chest. Concerned, I shut the bathroom door and went over.

"Is everything okay?" I said, touching her shoulder.

She didn't acknowledge my presence in any way. What could be the matter? Not the baby's cries – Rita seemed oblivious to them. The room appeared to be in order too. Then I happened to glance at the television.

It took me some time to recognise the house as mine; I'm not used to seeing anything so familiar on the news. My front garden was floodlit in the dark, though not too well, as if car headlights were trained on it. Beyond the birch tree huddled a group of men in suit pants, shirts and ties, with folders in their hands, and they seemed to be conferring with one another, right there on my front lawn.

Police.

My heart shrivelled inside my chest.

The picture changed to another house, similarly half-lit, with a man and a woman in navy blue uniforms wheeling a gurney towards an ambulance parked in the driveway. The gurney carried a long zippered bag. Four policemen in uniform complete with utility belts and holstered guns came out the front door, following the paramedics. At last, I recognised the house as the Whitmore's, and knew, with a sinking feeling in my guts, what was inside that long bag lying motionless on the gurney.

A detective appeared on-screen for a few moments, enclosed by a tight knot of reporters with their outstretched microphones and tape recorders.

The picture switched to a long shot of the Whitmore house from across the road, zooming in through shrubbery, this time featuring Mr Whitmore getting led from the door by two people, one on either side of him. His hands over his face, he sagged and swayed and stumbled along like a drunk. The people helping him negotiate his own front steps had to keep him upright. Oh, a harrowing sight.

And in a form of irresistible torture, I had to imagine what it must have been like for Mr Whitmore coming home from the supermarket last night, perhaps with milk and bread, perhaps with after-dinner snacks like chocolate and potato chips, calling out, *Honey I'm home*, or something along those lines, walking through the dead quiet of the house, expecting to find his wife and child as he had left them only minutes before, finding instead the bloodied bed, the empty bassinet. Which had he spotted first? Regardless, he would have pulled back the doona, wouldn't he? Seen his wife's ruined skull, her spattered brains? Yes, of course, and he would have started screaming. A chill closed around me as I remembered the abhorrent sound of those screams.

On the television appeared a colour photograph of a wan Mrs Whitmore hugging Abby cheek to cheek, probably taken at the hospital soon after Abby's birth. Next, footage of the Whitmore house in daylight, the property hemmed in yellow police tape, while a reporter wearing a smartly pressed suit stood on the footpath and gestured with both hands to emphasise whatever the hell he was saying.

"Give me the remote," I said to Rita. "I need the sound turned up."

She didn't answer.

Another colour photograph flashed onto the screen, this time of my face.

My *face*!

To be precise, it was my drivers licence photo, beaming across hundreds of thousands of televisions throughout Victoria; maybe even the whole country. It stabbed me in a disorientating jolt, as if I'd stepped outside of reality into a bizarre otherworld. However, the weirdness didn't last. As I leaned close to the set, scrutinising my own image, the only reaction I had was to observe that my hair appeared to be thinning at the front. Nothing else came to mind. My coolness surprised me in a mild, indifferent sort of way, and then pleased me greatly. It meant:

No more crying.

No more dizzy spells.

No more vomiting.

No more carrying on like a sissy boy getting a whipping from his angry, disappointed, hateful father.

Oh yes – Ronald Brian Spooner was going to handle this situation *like a man*.

"The remote," I said, louder this time, holding out my hand.

Rita grabbed the device from the floor and gave it to me. Instead of disengaging the 'mute' button, I switched off the television altogether. She turned her ashen face towards me, her mouth dropping open in surprise and silent protest. I smiled what felt like a debonair, cocky grin, and, reaching down, ran my fingers through her hair. In a movement that almost broke my heart, she momentarily leaned her cheek into my palm and closed her eyes, the tension gone from her face, as if my very presence was a great comfort, as if I was someone she could rely on.

She's still my woman, I realised, grateful and shocked.

"I've gotta take care of Lulu," Rita said. "She's dirty. Could you get me a nappy and some wipes?"

I did, and made fresh coffees while she changed the baby. Santa's insane advice rolled around in my head. How could I kill Rita when I loved her? It failed to make sense. Torn, I decided to concentrate on nothing but drinking my coffee. The perfect solution would come to me, I was sure. Hadn't the omens of the day steered me right so far? I checked my watch. We had an hour until check out: plenty of time yet.

The baby's cries dialled down into fretful, unhappy grizzles. Rita lifted the baby into her arms and hugged it close, kissing at its neck. Then she turned to me and said, "The news report showed your licence plate number."

I shrugged, gulping at my coffee.

"When we checked in last night," she added, "the motel owner recorded your licence plate number in the register."

Fingers numb, I clattered my cup onto the bedside table. "So the police know we're here?"

"If the motel owners have called them, yeah. But it could be the owners haven't seen the news, or if so, they haven't checked their register yet. Look, any way you cut it, we've got to get out of here now, right now. Please tell me you got your car."

"Yes," I lied, not bothering to correct her that my vehicle is, in fact, a ute. "And I got the plates too."

Beaming, she rushed over and kissed me promptly, a hard, wet smack on the mouth.

"Quick, pack our shit into the car," she said, putting down the baby on one of the single beds. "I have to give Lulu some milk before we leave or she'll keep bawling."

As Rita busied herself at the bench with its kettle, formula and bottles, and while the baby snivelled and whimpered, I started moving our bags, boxes and my single suitcase over by the front door. What other option did I have? I couldn't take our belongings outside to the empty car parking space, could I? But this lame ruse would only delay the truth for a few minutes. Then what? My mind spun in mud.

By sheer fluke, I happened to glance at the window in time to spot a late-model Commodore sedan pass along the driveway. Another late-model Commodore followed, and another. I knew what that meant. The breath seemed to wedge itself sideways in my windpipe.

Police.

The option of killing Rita in a deserted location was now off the table. Thanks, Santa – thanks for nothing. I grabbed the door handle, tightened my grip until my fingers hurt, pasted on a smile. I'd show empty hands, I'd be agreeable. There'd be no need for them to beat me. Absolutely no need.

"What are you doing, Ronnie?"

I looked around. Rita, stalled in the middle of the room gripping a bottle of baby formula, was levelling slitted eyes at me.

"Why aren't you packing the car?" she added, her gaze shifting around our lousy sleeping quarters, checking the windows, the doors, as if she could smell encroaching danger.

Oh, you're quite the crafty vixen, I figured grimly, nodding. How many times have you got yourself in – and out – of situations like this? *If the coppers busted in here, I'd collapse into tears and cling to them in relief because I'm your hostage, you get it?* That's what she had told me earlier in this very room. *By the time I get through telling my side of the story,* she had said, gloating, *everyone in the world is going to hate your guts.*

What about my side of the story? Who is going to believe me, I despaired, while Rita, seasoned liar, is shooting off her silver-tongued mouth? How many other men, lonely and foolish, had already taken the fall for her crimes?

The baby mewled. Both Rita and I were motionless; yet, for a brief instant, it felt like the motel room was an arena and we were circling each other, weighing each other up, waiting for the other to make a move.

We both jumped as the motel phone began ringing.

Rita said, "Who the fuck could that be?"

Belying the fresh wave of anxiety that had dried out my mouth, I smiled placatingly, made a shushing gesture at her, and picked up the handset.

"Hello?" I said.

21

Rita snatched the phone away, barking into the mouthpiece, "Yes, what is it, what do you want?" After a pause, she added, "Forget the mushrooms, I don't care, all right? Just forget it."

She hung up.

"Was that the motel owner calling about breakfast?" I said.

"That's what the bitch reckoned, but there's something else going on, and I don't like it." She picked up the baby and slipped the bottle's teat into its mouth, heading to the door. "Let's go."

"Ah," I said, sitting down on a bed and steepling my hands. "Now here's the thing. The ute is gone."

She whirled around. "Gone? What do you mean? Gone where?"

"Stolen, I imagine. It's no longer where I parked it. I walked back."

Carefully, deliberately, reining herself in, she crossed the room and perched on the very edge of the wing chair. Time passed. The baby sucked greedily at the bottle. Rita continued to look at me with blank, empty eyes. Neither of us spoke.

"Okay, we're through," she said.

"What?"

"I don't want to be with you any more. It's over."

My high, peeping laugh choked its way out. "We're breaking up?"

"Lulu and me are going to Queensland, but not you. Understand? You can do whatever the fuck you want."

The pain felt surprisingly physical, a giant's fist squeezing my heart, crushing my lungs. It took me some time to find my voice. "I thought you loved me."

"Hah. Love doesn't mean shit."

The last drops of milk gurgled from the bottle. Rita put the bottle on the bedside table, lifted the baby, patted its back.

Sweat began to bead my hairline. Was Rita bluffing? I couldn't be sure.

"Tell me something," I said. "And I want you to be honest, completely honest, no matter what. Can you do that?"

She didn't reply.

"This whole... thing between us," I said, gesturing a shape in the air with my hands, trying to illustrate, where words failed, the totality of what we had been through together. "This thing meant the world to me. Did you feel the same way? Or were you using me to get what you wanted? I have to know. Please. One way or the other, I have to know."

Her flat, expressionless eyes considered me for a few moments longer. Then she laid the baby on the other bed, went to her bulky hessian bag, hauled its strap over one shoulder, and at the bench, stuffed the formula tin, a couple of baby bottles, the half-empty bag of nappies, and the container of wet wipes into the bag's maw.

"What are you doing?" I said.

She wouldn't say anything, as if I wasn't even in the room. Her casual attitude gutted me as thoroughly as a fillet knife. As she walked towards the baby on the bed, I leapt up and clutched her wrist.

"Let me go," she hissed, trying to pull away.

"Rita, wait, the police are here."

And that stopped her. Stopped her like a bullet.

"Police?" she said, eyes bulging. "Where?"

"Right here, in the car park. Probably in reception too."

"You're lying."

"Fine." I released her wrist. "Have it your way."

She turned to the baby as if to pick it up, as if she intended on waltzing out of here and abandoning me, after everything I had done for her, after everything I had sacrificed. I grabbed her arm.

"You're not leaving," I said. "Not now. Not ever."

And right there, shockingly, for the very first time, in her fern-green irises with the tawny flecks, I saw fear.

Fear!

Of me, Ronald Brian Spooner: lifelong loser, neighbourhood joke. No-one had ever been frightened of me before. Who would have thought it possible? The intoxicating sight of Rita's fear both daunted and electrified, shooting adrenaline along every limb, kicking my heart into my mouth, swamping me with feelings I can't name or even try to explain.

She dropped her hessian bag and, lunging, snatched up the nearest bedside lamp. With the other hand, she yanked the cord from the wall-socket and brandished the lamp overhead. Goggling at this unexpected development, I realised she intended to clobber me with the lamp. Amazing. I had somehow passed from known reality into some other version where anything seemed possible.

My backhander caught her on the point of her chin, wheeling her around, making her drop the lamp. Before she could recover, I slid my arm about her neck. Her windpipe nestled snugly against the crook of my elbow.

"Stop it," I said, wrapping my other arm about her waist. "Don't fight me."

Rita kept thrashing. Why wouldn't she listen? All she had to do was stop, and I would have let her go.

We struggled on. Memories of other times when we had been in almost this exact same position came to mind. For example, one night in my kitchen, while I was hugging her from behind, she had shoved her bottom against my groin, signalling her intent. We had just eaten dinner – grilled lamb chops, green salad with olive oil and balsamic dressing, buttered white bread rolls – and were about to go into the backyard to sit in our respective deckchairs side-by-side, ready to share the experience of Mrs Whitmore, who had been, at that stage, still as fecund as a ripe fruit. Heady times.

"Oh, Rita," I whispered at her ear, pushing my erection against her coccyx, "I love you. I'm nothing without you."

But she wouldn't cease kicking her heels into my shinbones, gouging her fingers at my eyes. I tightened my arm about her throat and lifted her clear off the floor as her legs flailed and scissored wildly. Perhaps Mrs Whitmore in her death throes had kicked much the same way, I mused. Rita's legs finally slackened and dropped, twitching. She began to feel heavy in my arms.

"That's my good girl," I murmured, pressing my cheek against hers.

A knock sounded at the door.

"Not now, thank you," I called out.

"It's your breakfast, Mr and Mrs Andrews."

"Fine. Just leave it out there by the door, I'll get it later."

"But the eggs and bacon will get cold."

"Yes, that's okay, thank you. Put the food down and go away, please."

I heard a key scrabbling in the lock. The door swung open.

I caught a glimpse of the motel owner – an impression of a mountainous blonde beehive and dark-framed spectacles – before unseen hands wrenched her back from the doorway at great speed, like a shepherd's crook yanking a cartoon character off-stage. That's the only reason why I was laughing when police stormed the room.

By their military-style uniforms, bulletproof vests and hard hats, I recognised them as the Special Operations Group, the elite tactical division of the Victorian Police. How very flattering; no ordinary beat cops for the likes of Ronnie and Rita.

In a single moment, the law swarmed me, took Rita from me, wrestled me to the ground. Someone put their knee at the back of my neck.

A gruff male voice said, "Ronald Brian Spooner?"

"Yes, sir," I muttered, my face squashed against the carpet. "Please be careful of her. She'll attack you with a lamp."

Someone patted me down.

"You armed?" the voice added.

"That's ridiculous," I said, chuckling. What sort of man did they take me for?

My wrists were forced behind my back and cuffed. Hands fitted into my armpits and hauled me onto my feet. The two Special Operations Group officers flanking me were tall and large, kitted out like gridiron football players, both with the same professionally inscrutable expression. Neither smiled back at me.

Astonished, I peered about. Dozens of officers in various uniforms jammed the motel suite, filing in, filing out, standing singly or in groups, talking on radios, mobile phones, and to each other; every one of them looking stern and purposeful, smug and self-congratulatory, making such a fuss and palaver for us, for *me*, a man who normally means nothing to anyone. How bizarre.

A small crowd of officers surrounded Rita, who lay immobile on the floor.

"Rita," I said. "It's over. The police are here."

She didn't answer.

By the bathroom door, a young officer in the standard blue police uniform, hair cut so short that the pinkness of his scalp gleamed through every strand, had the sleeping baby cradled awkwardly against his chest like he'd never held a child before.

"Goodbye, Abby Rose Whitmore," I said, but felt nothing for the little beast that had ruined my life.

The officer snarled, "Shut up, you sick bastard," and ducked out of the motel room as if he was worried my gaze could burn holes in the baby.

Galvanised, the SOGs dragged me to the wing chair and sat me down, hard. They pressed hands on my shoulders, presumably to prevent my getting up and trying to flee. What they failed to appreciate: I had nowhere to go.

A few minutes later, you and the other homicide detectives arrived.

And that's it. Everything that happened, the whole story from the beginning.

Except for one last thing.

The police officers that were huddled around Rita fell back to allow paramedics enough room. In a flurry of activity, the paramedics started taking Rita's pulse, lifting her eyelids, wrapping one of her arms with a blood pressure cuff, ripping open plastic bags full of equipment, readying hypodermic syringes, medicine bottles, some type of gas mask.

"Rita," I yelled, impatient and angry at her charade. "Stop playing possum and get up."

Of course, she didn't. She couldn't.

I would cry for her, but I'm too tired.

What time is it?

God, I've been talking for hours. May I have another coffee?

ABOUT THE AUTHOR

Deborah Sheldon's short fiction has appeared in many well-respected journals such as *Quadrant, Island, Page Seventeen, Tincture Journal* and *[untitled]*, and also in various anthologies including *Hard Labour* (Crime Factory), *The One That Got Away* (Dark Prints Press), *The Day Death Wore Boots* (Alfie Dog Fiction UK), and *100 Lightnings* (Paroxysm Press). Her literary collection, *300 Degree Days and Other Stories* (Ginninderra Press), was published in 2014. In February 2015, Satalyte Publishing will release her collection, *Mayhem: Selected Stories*.

She has two novels slated for publication in 2015 and 2016 respectively. Other writing credits include TV scripts such as Neighbours and Australia's Most Wanted; feature articles for national magazines; stage and radio plays; award-winning medical writing; and non-fiction books for Reed Books and Random House.

Deb lives in Melbourne.

Visit her at www.deborahsheldon.wordpress.com

Printed in Australia
AUOC02n1739200315
266496AU00007B/7/P